
★

Could the judge be in the car?

Sharyn looked at the garage floor. The concrete was alive with every kind of tool and device as well as broken glass and live wires but she could see a path where someone had dragged something across it. She would have to stay low and try to reach the judge to get him out.

If the pattern played out and he was either dead or unconscious from a blow to the back of the head, she knew it was going to be more difficult. The judge was a big man. She wasn't sure if she could carry him to safety. Unfortunately, she didn't have much time to plan what she could do to get them both out of there. Any plan could lead to both their deaths.

But she didn't plan on dying that day. She had way too much to do. She tried to keep her head low but the heat and smoke were intense. She only had a few moments to get out of there and take the judge with her.

★

THE LAST
TO REMEMBER

JOYCE & JIM LAVENE

TORONTO • NEW YORK • LONDON
AMSTERDAM • PARIS • SYDNEY • HAMBURG
STOCKHOLM • ATHENS • TOKYO • MILAN
MADRID • WARSAW • BUDAPEST • AUCKLAND

Recycling programs
for this product may
not exist in your area.

THE LAST TO REMEMBER

A Worldwide Mystery/September 2011

First published by Avalon Books

ISBN-13: 978-0-373-26769-9

Printed in U.S.A.

For our family,
whose continued support
and cheerleading efforts keep us going!

PROLOGUE

IT HAD BEEN A long day for Mary Alice Fine. She took her job as assistant to the County Resource Officer for Public Schools seriously. Even when they moved the resource officer's office to the drafty old training school building. She tried not to complain about the lack of facilities or criticize the county policy of using every square foot of space it already owned, despite its condition. If the county didn't want to build, far be it for her to question their judgment. Surely they were intelligent people who knew more than she did, even if she had worked the job every day of her life for the past thirty years!

When the snow started falling at about 3:00 p.m., the rest of the assistants in the office left for the day. Mary Alice stayed. At five minutes of 5:00, when the late-autumn snowstorm had become a blizzard, she was still there, filing the last of her reports. At the stroke of five, she pulled on her jacket and picked up her pocketbook. She shut down the lights in the preternatural darkness and locked the door behind her.

She was slipping and sliding across the icy parking lot to her car when she realized that there was a light on in the old chapel.

Anyone with less of an eye for detail wouldn't have noticed. Anyone less dedicated would have turned away. Since Mary Alice wasn't afflicted with either of these faults, she started across the old stone bridge that crossed the highway. It was slippery there, too. She had to keep her hand on the stone wall that enclosed the walkway to keep her balance.

Mary Alice knew she would have to report this to the resource officer. After all, if the maintenance crews left the lights on everywhere they went, the county would never be able to afford a new building! She crossed the bridge slowly and finally reached the chapel door. She inched it open, the rarely used hinges protesting in the cold. Snow blew in across the floor at her feet.

She looked up, put her hand on the light switch, and froze. Mary Alice had never screamed before, that she could recall, but she did herself proud at that moment. Her voice cut through the chapel and the old training school campus like the sharp edge of a knife.

ONE

"WHAT DO YOU MEAN, you don't know where she is?" Nick asked angrily.

Ernie Watkins shrugged his thin shoulders and touched his new mustache. "I mean that I don't know where she is," he answered sharply. "She's with Lennie, okay? She spends a lot of time with Lennie these days."

Nick paced the chapel floor and thrust his hand through his thick, dark hair. Snow crystals outlined the faint traces of gray that shot through the strands. "What do we know about this guy, anyway?"

"We know he's sharp, he's young, and he's ambitious," Ernie replied with a small smile curling his lip. "What's wrong, Nick? Getting scared?"

"Scared?" Nick demanded, turning to face him. "Of *what?*"

Ernie shook his head. "I think we both know *what,* friend. Question is, *what* are you gonna do about it?"

Nick Thomopolis buried his hands in his coat pockets and hunched down into the warmth it afforded him. "Nothing," he responded finally. "She'll have to do what she wants." He stomped his feet on the stone floor. "It's too cold for this time of year."

"Nick—" Ernie began, only to stop abruptly as he heard Sharyn's voice coming through the darkness that surrounded the little chapel.

Sharyn Howard walked through the chapel door, surprised to see Ernie and Nick there. She wasn't in uniform. She'd been at a city fund-raiser when the call had come in for her. She'd lost ten pounds before the event so that she could wear a new midnight-blue sequined gown. It, and the three-inch heels she wore, made her feel slender and graceful for a change. Her hair had been growing out for a while. It was penny bright and pulled back from her face with a sapphire clip.

"Ernie." She nodded to her deputy. "Nick. I'm surprised you're here."

"Let me see," Nick began sarcastically. "Someone found a dead body. I'm the medical examiner for this county. Why would I be here again?"

Sharyn frowned at him. Their relationship was always shifting. She couldn't figure out why he was so nice sometimes and so disgusting other times. He did his job well. She just couldn't figure him personally.

"We met Jeremy in the parking lot. He's on the way with the forensics team. So I thought you weren't here. Wasn't that why I begged the city council to hire you an assistant? So you didn't have to work so hard?"

"Jeremy is the assistant medical examiner," Nick reminded her. "In this state, that means he can perform autopsies and help investigate crime scenes, but the official medical examiner has to be at all crime scenes, regardless of snow or dark." He glanced at her. "Or even parties."

"I wouldn't call the fund-raiser a party exactly," the man beside Sharyn spoke up. He dwarfed her. He was tall and good-looking. His dark skin was smooth. His dark eyes were clear, taking in the scene before him in the chapel. His broad shoulders had wedged him through some clenches with the Atlanta Falcons when he'd played for them.

But Lennie Albert wanted more from life than a football career. He'd played for two years but now he was working as a sheriff's deputy and finishing law school. He wanted to be the next DA of Diamond Springs, his hometown. "There was more skirmishing going on there than at a Monday-night football game."

Nick's eyes rested where Lennie's dark hand still held Sharyn's arm. "I'll bet."

Sharyn moved away from her companion, not noticing as Ernie and Nick exchanged glances over the top of her head. "Never mind the fund-raiser anyway." She put an end to that discussion. "What can you tell me about what happened here?"

Jeremy Lambert, the new assistant medical examiner from Atlanta, swept into the room with the forensics team and a body bag. "I can tell you that the victim is a child, from the bone structure and development. I'd say about eight or ten. I think it was a boy. From the looks of the dirt and sediment around the bones, I'd say he was buried for a while and recently dug up and placed here."

Nick shrugged and lay back on a wooden pew, resting his long legs on the back of the seat.

Sharyn glanced at him. She didn't expect anything else from him in that mood. He'd been in a foul mood for weeks but that was nothing new either. When she'd first become sheriff, she didn't think he'd stay with the county. He'd actually given his resignation once but then changed his mind. She never knew what to expect from him. Except a hard time.

She'd thought something was happening between them. Something that had improved their working life, but she'd obviously been wrong because he was back to his old nasty self the past few weeks.

The skeleton of the dead boy was hanging from the rugged wooden cross in the front of the old church. Small, pathetic arms reached out from the body. He was loosely roped to the cross, the skull resting just above the breastbone on the wooden head of Jesus. The small eye sockets stared vacantly across the room.

Jeremy Lambert looked at Nick. He was a tall man in his late forties with a stocky build and thick glasses. He had recently joined the county medical examiner's office and had a disturbing habit of trying to show up his boss. "Did you want to finish telling the sheriff about this?" he asked politely.

"No, please, continue," Nick told him. "I'm just here so the sheriff isn't lonely. You know, not enough men in her life."

Ernie shook his head and smiled. He stomped his feet on the stone floor to keep warm.

"Well." Jeremy debated if he should actually continue.

"Go on," Sharyn encouraged him. "It's nice for someone to take their job seriously."

"All right." He glanced at Nick again then reached up with his gloved hands and removed the skull. The rest of the team of forensics students were removing and carefully tagging and placing the bones into the case. "You can see from this that the skull received blunt-force trauma. The back is crushed in. It was probably bad enough to kill the child."

Sharyn sighed. "I can see from the discoloration of the bones that they aren't new."

Nick clapped his hands a few times, then subsided.

"Probably at least twenty years old or more," Jeremy said, carefully holding the skull.

Sharyn moved closer to observe the skull. "And male? Since we're standing on the grounds of an old boys' school, I suppose it isn't surprising."

She looked around the old chapel that had been created out of rough stone quarried right there at the school. The pews were rough wood, slightly uneven, some a little longer than others. Generations of boys coming to church there every day had worn the gray stone floor smooth. The big oak cross at the front was cut by the boys' hands. The figure of Jesus was little more than a silhouette with a head. The addition of the boy's bones made the cross gruesome.

There was only one small window cut into the stone. It was at least eight feet high and covered in bars. Whoever brought the skeleton into the chapel had to come through the heavy oak door. It was possible that it was just a prank, leaving the skeleton there. If they could find fingerprints, the chances were that they belonged to some teenager who lived close by. The old school campus was a magnet for teens and vagrants.

"I think the question would be why someone put the bones here. They weren't here earlier today when the building was serviced," Ernie added. "Ms. Fine walked across the bridge in the snowstorm because the light was left on. I think we should assume that someone wanted these bones to be found."

"That's obvious." Lennie joined in on the conversation. "Maybe some prints will turn up. This place doesn't look like it's used much. Whoever put it here was bound to leave something behind."

"I'll put you in charge of that, Lennie," Sharyn told him. "Hang around with forensics and let me know what's going on here. Where is Mary Alice, Ernie?"

"I sent her home after I took her statement. She was pretty shaken up, Sheriff. I told her we'd call if we needed her again."

"Okay."

"The bones will have to be sent to Raleigh to be examined," Nick said, still lying on the pew. "We can't do that work here."

"Actually," Jeremy began, licking his chapped lips in the cold, "I *could*—"

"The state won't *let* us do that work here," Nick continued flatly. "We're required to send them to Raleigh."

"There won't be any point in checking the grounds till this snow clears," Ernie stated. "By then, any tracks are gonna be gone, too, Sheriff. I'll take a look, though. I'm bound to know this campus better than most people."

"You might be surprised," Jeremy said smoothly.

"I've studied this place. I've done hours of research about it. It was the first of its kind, you know. A place to send young boys who would otherwise have gone to jail with adults. They worked hard and grew their own food, even made their own clothes. This place saved a lot of lives."

"Yeah, well, it ruined a lot of them, too," Ernie said gruffly. "It might've been a noble idea at the beginning but it ended up just being a jail like any other."

"But the boys learned so much here," Jeremy persisted. "They learned a skill. Did you know that this chapel and some of the houses where the boys lived, along with the bridge outside, were built by boys who went to school here? They learned to be stonemasons and woodworkers, carpenters, and draftsmen. They were given a second chance."

"A second chance for what?" Ernie argued outright, glaring at Jeremy. "Living through a nightmare after they'd just been in a nightmare? I never knew anyone who went here who didn't come out a little tougher and meaner because of the way they were treated."

"It's not bad to be tough," Lennie joined in. "Tough survives."

"Maybe tougher was good, Ernie," Jeremy continued. "Maybe those boys needed to learn to be tough.

I've seen pictures of them building that bridge out-side. They took some of that with them."

"Sheriff." Ernie turned to her suddenly, disgusted with the discussion. "If there's nothing more, I'd like to get back to Annie before the storm gets worse. David, Ed, and Joe are all out on the roads. I told them to call if they need a hand. I don't see where there's anything to do here until the sun comes out tomorrow and burns off this snow."

"Sure, Ernie," Sharyn said slowly, surprised by his vehement disapproval of the training school that most of the state admired. The county was trying to pre-serve the old buildings as historic landmarks. There had even been calls for the school to be brought back to help today's troubled youths. "We'll probably need you at the office to help man the phones later."

"That's fine. I'll be at home," he said, walking out of the chapel. The snow was still falling in large wet clumps at the doorway.

"We'll finish up here," Jeremy told her. "I'll get my report to you ASAP."

"Thanks, Jeremy," Sharyn said, glancing at Nick. "I appreciate your willingness to help."

"I'll walk you back out to your car," Lennie vol-unteered, reaching to take Sharyn's arm again. "With those shoes, you shouldn't be walking on this rough terrain in a snowstorm."

They all looked down at her strappy blue heels.

Sharyn felt foolish standing there as the sheriff of Diamond Springs dressed that way. Her father wouldn't have approved. Her grandfather would probably have shot her. Both men had taken their jobs as sheriff very seriously.

When the call came in that night, she didn't know what had happened. Otherwise, she would've gone home and changed.

"That's okay," Nick said, standing suddenly and intercepting Lennie's hand. His hand settled firmly on Sharyn's arm. "It looks like you've got your job cut out for you here. My assistant is taking care of the rest, so I might as well walk out with the sheriff."

Lennie shrugged his very wide shoulders, emphasizing his broad chest, powerful body, and the close fit of his tuxedo. "Sure, Nick. That works, too. Just didn't want Sharyn to walk out unescorted."

Nick ground his teeth. "I'll escort the *sheriff.*"

Lennie smiled and inclined his head toward Sharyn. "I had a good time tonight. Thanks for the opportunity to meet the mayor and the council."

"Sure thing," Sharyn replied, wondering what was going on between the two men. For that matter, what was going on between Jeremy and Ernie? Maybe it was the weather, she decided. Maybe it raised testosterone levels to dangerous highs. "I'll see you later."

"You bet."

Sharyn was being steadily drawn to the chapel

door by Nick's hold on her arm. She finally gave in to it and was propelled out of the tiny chapel at break-neck speed. When they reached the bridge, she tried to dig in her feet but the snow was drifting across her frozen toes, making her shiver.

"Hold on," she yelled at him. "You were supposed to keep me from falling, not push me off the side of the bridge."

Nick stopped abruptly. "Oh? Would Lennie have done a better job of escorting you, *Sharyn?*"

"What *is* your problem this time, Nick?" she demanded, facing him even though it meant that snow was pelting her.

The streetlight that illuminated the bridge was shining into her face. A big, soft, wet snowflake plopped onto her nose. Before she could move it, he had taken his finger and pushed it away. "Come on," he said in a gruff voice, taking her arm again. "You're gonna die of pneumonia out here, dressed like that."

"Is that it?" she wondered. "You have a problem with me not being in uniform?"

"I don't have a problem with you being out of uniform," he replied, calmly continuing to walk. More slowly, this time. His hand was more secure on her arm as he felt her foot slide on the ground.

"You resent me not being here sooner?"

"I don't resent you."

"Then what?" She forced him to release her arm again. "I thought we had some understanding between us that we were going to get along now. I thought we were past all this stupid stuff and we could work together professionally."

"Sharyn," he began, equally as angry. He took another few steps into the icy parking lot and heard her quick intake of breath as she stalked after him. He turned in time to catch her in his arms as she slipped on the ice; she would have fallen to the hard pavement beneath the blanket of sparkling white snow.

"Sorry," she said quietly, glad to feel his arms go around her. His hands were strong and warm at her waist beneath the thin layer of her matching blue velvet cloak. She shivered in the icy wind that swept by them and looked up into his face.

"Sharyn," he said again, this time in a voice that wasn't angry but mellow like old brandy. "My only problem is you. Just you."

She stared at him, wishing she could see his face more clearly in the streetlight. "I don't understand, Nick. Why am I such a problem for you?"

It seemed to her that it was only a matter of seconds before he had her bundled into her car and he was closing the door. Without answering her question.

"I suppose that's the big problem, Sharyn. If you understood, it might be different."

"But why can't you explain?" she began. "Why can't you just tell me and we might be able to resolve it?"

"Good night, Sheriff," he said, and closed the car door on her next words.

She watched him walk carefully to his own car, start the engine, and drive away while she was still sitting there, trying to figure out what had just happening between them.

Nick was Nick, she supposed, putting her key into the ignition and starting the car. For the two years that she had been sheriff of Diamond Springs, he had been a thorn in her side.

Her father, the previous sheriff, had worked with Nick and had nothing but praise for the man. But when Sharyn had won the special election following her father's murder at a local convenience store, it had been different for her. He was an excellent medical examiner and he had helped her through some tough spots, but their personal relationship bordered on animosity.

Sharyn drove home carefully though the thick, wet blanket of snow. She put thoughts of Nick behind her. Ernie was right, of course. In the Uwharrie area of North Carolina, the snow never lasted. The sun would come out for a few hours and the raging blizzard from the night before would vanish. Sometime tomorrow, they would be able to find the spot where the boy's grave had been robbed, probably from the old cemetery that belonged to the school grounds.

A death at the boys' school would have been reported, she considered. The school had been closed for the past ten years. If Jeremy was right about the time frame, there should be some mention of the death in the school, as well as the police records. She would have Ernie check the files for anything mentioned. She knew that the school had once policed their own but not in the past twenty years. Her father or grandfather would have been involved in handling it.

The boy was probably killed accidentally. The boys there had done some difficult things. Hard labor and farm work where a child could have been injured in that extreme way. That should have been reported, too. There should be a record of the boy's death at the sheriff's office.

Sharyn drove back to her house before starting toward the office. It was getting late and the storm was getting worse, but she wasn't going to the office in her evening gown and blue satin shoes. She didn't want to see anyone else react to her outfit.

A long black limo was parked in her drive when she pulled down the street to her house. She frowned. It was the senator. He and her mother had grown continually closer in the past few months. She had begun avoiding her mother, since they only seemed to argue about the fact. Faye Howard was right. She was certainly old enough to make her own judgments. Sharyn didn't want to see her mother left alone after her father's death. She just wished she had picked anyone but Caison Talbot!

Sharyn let herself into the house through the back door, slogging through the heavy snow, ruining her shoes, so that she could avoid seeing her mother and the senator. She managed to get through the kitchen but her mother's sharp ears heard her footsteps in the hall.

"Sharyn?" Faye called. "Are you going to come in and speak to us? Or just sneak in and out?"

Sharyn had had the same problem as a teenager. Her mother had superhuman hearing. The few times she'd tried to sneak in or out, she'd been caught and punished. Sharyn had been a very plain child, so she wasn't sneaking out to meet a boy. More often than not, she was sneaking out to look at the stars with her telescope or go for a swim in the lake.

Removing her shoes, Sharyn walked into the formal living room. Her mother was there in evening clothes with the senator in a tuxedo beside her. They were both drinking glasses of wine and sitting on the good green sofa that was covered in plastic. Faye's face was flushed and her hair was a little mussed. Sharyn didn't want to speculate about what they had been doing.

"Mom," she acknowledged her. "Senator."

She'd seen them at the fund-raiser that night but managed to maneuver Lennie between them. Those broad shoulders took up a lot of room. Caison was the senator for their district. He spent too much time on his home turf, as far as Sharyn was concerned. She would've liked him better if he spent more time at the capitol.

"Sharyn," her mother said with a smile, her hand in the senator's hand.

"Sheriff," Senator Talbot addressed her. "We thought we might see you at the fund-raiser. Your mother was very disappointed when you managed to sneak by without speaking to us."

"There was no sneaking involved," Sharyn told him plainly. "I don't sneak anywhere."

"Then what was that you were just doing, honey?" her mother wondered. "You were hoping to avoid us again, weren't you?"

"I have to go," Sharyn told them, turning away.

"Big case?" the senator asked. "I saw you and that Albert fella leave early."

"I don't think so." She shrugged. "I just need to go to the office."

"Of course, Sharyn," her mother answered, remarkably pleasantly. "But later, we have to talk, dear."

"Yes, your mother and I have something important to tell you."

"Kristie is supposed to be home this weekend," Sharyn told them both. "Maybe we can talk then."

She hurried to her room and closed the door. It wasn't the first time that she'd heartily considered moving into her own place. She was certainly old enough and she could afford it. She'd stayed more because she didn't want her mother to be alone while Kristie was away at school. She loved her mother. They just couldn't seem to get along.

She certainly didn't love Caison Talbot. The man was an attention pig. Always on the lookout for the next media blitz that might work for him. He tried to manipulate the county into being his own little plantation. But she suspected her mother might love him. Or at least, think that she was in love with him.

Sharyn stepped out of her new dress and hung it carefully on the hanger. She took out her uniform, freshly pressed and laundered. Even losing ten pounds didn't help the way it looked on her. It gave her already squarish body and face the look of a cereal box. The tan and brown did nothing for her color. But she'd fought hard to have the right to wear it after her father's death. She tucked in her shirt and added her holster and her grandfather's service revolver. The badge was shiny on her chest. It represented law and dignity and loyalty and honor. She stood for those things for the people of Diamond Springs and the surrounding county.

She put on her hat and picked up her warm jacket. The heavy work shoes felt good on her feet after the cold in her dress shoes. There was a time to be Cinderella, she told her appearance in the mirror. And there was a time to be the sheriff.

Carefully, she walked back out of the house through the kitchen. This time, her mother and the senator ignored her. She breathed a sigh of relief. She knew the senator would pick up on the skeleton in the chapel. He would find some way to spin it that looked good for him. She gritted her teeth when she thought about it.

The blizzard continued unabated. The roads were starting to show the effect. Plows would be out later but there weren't many of them. The area didn't get a lot of snow, even though it was in the mountains. Their elevation wasn't enough to stay any colder than the surrounding North Carolina countryside. It was only mid-October. They were still due for some nice fall weather.

She knew the television and radio announcers would be telling everyone to stay home. For the most part, everyone would listen. The roads were already empty, which was a blessing. The last thing they needed was a major pileup. Trying to get ambulances and medical personnel through a blizzard was almost impossible.

The problem came in when the power lines couldn't support the weight of the heavy, wet snow and collapsed. Power could be off for days and the city always went wild. When she was a kid, she'd loved it. No school. Lanterns and candles. Different food to eat in the dark with a roaring fire in the hearth.

As an adult, and especially as the sheriff, she dreaded it. People did the weirdest things during blackouts. It was all they could do to answer the phones and keep everyone calm. She eyed the drooping power lines with dismay. She might as well get ready for it, she decided. There was little chance it wouldn't happen.

She reached the city proper and parked inside the lot in the back of the office. Charlie, the impound man, was there. He waved to her and closed the gate behind her.

"Gonna lose the power, Sheriff," he told her without preamble.

"I know, Charlie," she agreed. "I'm glad you came in."

"Don't like the idea of losing anything while the lights are off," he responded. "Had to take care of what's here."

"Thanks, Charlie," she answered, recalling how he'd let her ride her bike through the gate and park it in the lot when her father was sheriff. She had loved trailing after her father at the office, listening to the meetings when he'd let her come.

She missed him. She stamped her foot on the tile to get rid of some of the clinging snow. He'd been gone only two years but it seemed like a lifetime. What would he have made of the bones in the chapel? she wondered. T. Raymond Howard had been a calm man, not given to being excited. He probably would've thought it was a prank and wouldn't have done anything except rebury the bones.

"Sheriff," Trudy greeted her at the door. "I was hoping you'd get here soon."

"The roads were pretty bad already or I would've been here sooner, Trudy," Sharyn explained. "Call in Ed and Joe. The streets were pretty empty. We might need them here if the power goes off. Go ahead and give Ernie a call, too."

"He's at Annie's," Trudy told her with a smile.

Sharyn smiled back. "I know. I'm happy for him, finding Annie again after all these years, too, Trudy. But we might need him."

"Okay. What about David?"

"Tell him to head in as soon as things look clear for any traffic. The plows should be through soon."

"Okay, Sheriff."

"Lennie is at the chapel with the forensics team. He should come back in after he's done," Sharyn told her assistant.

The front doors to the sheriff's office burst open at that moment, and a man, shivering and soaking wet with snow, threw himself on the floor.

"I'm guilty!" he screamed. "I'm here to confess my guilt."

The power chose that moment to go out. The room was black, then partially lit as the emergency lighting kicked in.

"Here we go again," Trudy said with a deep breath.

TWO

"WHAT'S IT ABOUT the power going off that brings out the kooks?" Trudy asked.

"The power wasn't off yet," Sharyn replied.

"He must have known it was going to happen."

There were already several emergency coordinators in the big room that was the main part of the sheriff's office. They froze in place as the emergency lighting came on. The room was ominously still.

"It's okay," Sharyn said as she and Trudy helped the man in the doorway to his feet. "This is emergency power," she explained to the room in general. "There's going to be a lot of people in here through the rest of the storm, so everybody just take a deep breath and do your job."

"I'll get him some coffee," Trudy volunteered when they had helped the man into a chair.

"Thanks, Trudy. I hope the emergency power covers that, too," Sharyn said, staying with the man.

Trudy nodded. "I'll put on another pot."

Sharyn sat beside the man who'd fallen in the doorway. He was a mess. Mud and snow and slush covered him. His face and hands were dirty and his hair was in his face but he looked vaguely familiar to her. The jeans he wore were in good condition and carried a brand name. His shirt was torn but seemed to be of good quality.

"Are you feeling better now?" she asked him, but there was no response. He continued to stare straight ahead. "Can you tell me your name?" She heard the doors open and close behind her.

"Hey, this looks like a sci-fi movie!" Ed proclaimed as he and Joe walked into the building. "Look at this lighting!"

"Special effects," Joe agreed. "Trudy!" he called. "Where's the sheriff?"

"Right here," Sharyn told him. She nodded to the man at her side. "He walked in off the street just before the power went out."

"Before?" Ed asked. "That's strange."

"What's wrong with him?" Joe wondered, leaning down close to him. He looked into the man's face. "Hey, it's Beau Richmond."

"No!" Ed disputed, looking into the man's face, too. "It is! It's Beau Richmond."

"Are you sure?" Sharyn asked, bringing a towel to where the man sat. She washed his face and pushed back his wild hair. "It is! Mr. Richmond, can you hear me?"

Beau Richmond was one of the county's most

prominent citizens. He'd been at the fund-raiser that night. There wasn't a person in Diamond Springs who didn't feel blessed by the man's presence there. His charitable awards and good deeds were legendary.

"Mr. Richmond?" Ed tried to get his attention. "Mr. Richmond, it's Ed Robinson. Do you remember me?"

The man stared ahead vacantly.

Ed grimaced. "I met him last year at a barbecue for the Little League. I thought he might remember."

Sharyn crouched down in front of him and took his icy hands in hers. "Mr. Richmond," she tried again. "It's Sheriff Howard. Remember? I saw you tonight at the fund-raiser. We spoke briefly."

Beau Richmond, who sat on the board of more companies than Sharyn had stock, swiveled his head to look at her. His eyes focused on her face, then he looked around him. "Help me, Sheriff."

"I'll be glad to, sir," she told him. "Tell me what the problem is." It was hard for her to imagine that this was the same man who'd been at the fund-raiser, telling jokes and holding hands with his beautiful young wife.

Trudy returned with a cup of hot coffee and a dry blanket. She gave him the coffee and wrapped the blanket around his shaking shoulders. "Oh, glory! Is that Beau Richmond?"

"Trudy," Sharyn whispered to her, "call his wife."

"Sheriff," Beau said in a stronger voice, once he had sipped the coffee, "I have to confess."

"To what, sir?" Sharyn asked, seeing Ed and Joe exchange looks out of the corner of her eye. David came in from the street, shaking with cold and muttering about the work.

"Murder, Sheriff."

"Sir," Sharyn cautioned the man, "maybe you'd better wait to say any more. We're all deputies of the court, Mr. Richmond. We can't pretend not to know whatever you tell us."

"I understand that, Sheriff Howard," Beau told her lucidly. "I apologize for the state I'm in but I have to tell the truth. I have to get someone to listen to me."

"Please don't tell me he murdered that fine young wife of his," Ed whispered.

Sharyn glared at him. "The phones are ringing off the hook, Ed. Why don't you and Joe go and see if you can help?"

"You need someone else to witness this, Sheriff," Joe argued. "In case he does really want to confess to something and wants to take it back later."

"That's true," she agreed as Lennie walked in through the front door. "Lennie, will you come over here, please?" She looked at Joe and Ed. "Now, you two can help on the phones."

Ed pretended to shoot her with his finger as they walked away.

"What's he got that we ain't?" Joe muttered.

Ed laughed. "The sheriff in his pocket?"

"Did you see Ernie on your way in?" she asked Lennie when he reached her side.

"No. Is there a problem?"

Sharyn considered the situation. She really didn't want to take a statement from Beau Richmond without a lawyer present, or at least someone from his family. She didn't want to be accused of taking advantage of his condition, whatever it was. Something was wrong with the man. Maybe the best thing to do would be to get an ambulance there to see to him.

"I don't know," she admitted, biting on her lip as she tried to decide her next course of action.

"Phones are out, Sheriff," Trudy came back and told her. "Emergency won't be on for a few minutes, they tell me. Want me to send David out?"

"No," Sharyn decided. "Give Lennie the address and let him go."

"Go where?" Lennie wondered.

"To Beau Richmond's house for his wife," she explained. "She's the nearest relative I can think of. Get her here as fast as you can. Trudy, call an ambulance for Beau. If we can get him out of here, I'll let you know," she promised Lennie.

"Okay," Lennie agreed. "Are you sure you wouldn't rather send David or Joe?"

Sharyn glanced at him. "Yes. Be careful. Let me know if anything is wrong with Mrs. Richmond."

The main office had become such a hive of activity that Sharyn decided to move Beau into the interrogation/conference room. It would be quiet there and the man might begin to think clearly again.

"Thank you, Sheriff," he said when they had made the move with Trudy's help. "Can I confess now?"

"To a murder?" Sharyn wondered.

"Yes."

"Mr. Richmond, there's an ambulance on the way for you. I sent a deputy for your wife." She turned and saw Ernie walk into the room. She didn't know if she had ever been happier to see another face. "Excuse me a minute, Mr. Richmond."

"All right. But I still want to confess."

Sharyn joined Ernie in the corner of the room. He looked disheveled. He wasn't wearing his uniform and had the look of a man who'd just woken up from a dream he hadn't wanted to leave. "Thanks for coming in, Ernie."

"Sure, Sheriff." He nodded at Beau. "What's the problem here?"

"He wants to confess to a murder," Sharyn explained. "He threw himself in here on the floor just before the power went off. Now he says he wants to confess."

"Is that Beau Richmond?" Ernie asked in disbelief.

She nodded. "I sent Lennie for his wife and had Trudy call for an ambulance. I was hoping you'd get here in case he did confess."

Ernie looked pleased. "You were?"

Sharyn looked at him steadily. "Ernie, you know I depend on you. But lately—"

"I know." He held up his hand. "I have a life besides the job."

She didn't want to argue. "Never mind. The question is, do we take his statement?"

He shrugged. "It's your decision, Sheriff. He seems clearheaded to me. It could be considered under duress but you've got an office full of people who could testify that you tried to get him not to confess."

Sharyn shrugged. "Which is something I wouldn't do with anyone except Beau Richmond."

Ernie looked at the other man. "It would seem that way to me."

"I want to confess now, Sheriff," Beau said again. "Should you have someone write this down?"

"I'll write it down, Beau," Ernie told him, taking out a small notebook. "If you have something to say, we'll listen."

"Good." Beau looked at Ernie and smiled. "Ernie! It's good to see you. You'll understand why I have to tell you this."

"All right, Beau. Just let me read you your rights first."

"Oh, I don't need those."

"But we do," Ernie told him.

Sharyn listened while Ernie read and explained Miranda to Beau.

The other man nodded and signed a waiver of his rights. "Can I confess now?"

"Go ahead, Mr. Richmond," Sharyn told him.

Beau Richmond closed his eyes then leaned forward on the table. "I killed a boy."

Sharyn heard Ernie's quick intake of breath. She knew how he felt. It was hard for her to believe anything so vile of Beau, unless it was an accident.

"Where did you kill him?" she asked him.

"At the school."

"What school?"

"The old training school. Jefferson."

Sharyn glanced at Ernie. He was totally focused on Beau, his brow furrowed intently. "When did you kill the boy?" she asked Beau.

"Forty years ago this night."

"What?" Sharyn asked abruptly.

Beau looked at her. "It was forty years ago. I was at the school because I quit going to the regular school. They caught me smoking some cigarettes I'd stolen from Goodwin's. You remember Goodwin's, Ernie? All the kids used to go there. We used to steal penny candy from him because his eyesight wasn't too good. Then we stole cigarettes when we got older. When that old man died, part of my childhood died with him."

"And you killed a boy?"

"That's right," one of the richest and most powerful men in the county told them. "His name was Michael Smith. He was small and we used to pick on him. Punch him once in a while. Kick him down the stairs. He was kind of slow so he could never really figure it out."

Sharyn sat back in her chair. "How did you kill him?"

"We were working on the bridge at the time. They made us do the new stonework. We got him to go there late one night and we hit him in the head and threw him down the embankment. We dug a little grave for him there and buried him under some leaves and stuff."

"The school officials never looked for him or found his body?" Sharyn persisted.

"They looked, I guess, but boys ran away every day. They never found him. Or at least, they never said they found him. I don't know why I didn't think about it after that but I just didn't. Not until recently.

Then I started to think about that little boy in the grave, cold and wet. No family. No one to claim him or to know where he was buried."

"You said 'we,'" Sharyn noted, surprised at Ernie's silence. "Who was with you?"

"I don't know," Beau answered quickly. "It doesn't matter. I was responsible. Now you can bury him. I want to pay for him to have a proper burial, Sheriff." He looked at her, his eyes keen on her face, filled with tears.

"All right," she agreed quietly. "Excuse us a minute, Mr. Richmond."

Sharyn stepped out of the room with Ernie. He handed her the notebook and pen.

"I can't do this, Sheriff."

"Ernie, we don't have much choice *now,* do we?"

"I do," Ernie said. "I think I should work on something else."

"What's wrong?" she wondered, seeing the despair on his face.

"I just can't help do this to a man who's done so much good for this community," he confessed, running his hand back through the sprig of hair on his head.

"But you said—"

"I know what I said," he replied angrily, raising his voice so that everyone looked at them. "I know what I said," he repeated more quietly. "I can't advise you on this, Sharyn. Don't ask me anything else, please."

He walked away and left her standing at the door, staring after him. Sharyn didn't hear Trudy call her name until she'd repeated it twice.

Ernie had called her Sharyn. In the middle of the office.

"I heard from Lennie at the Richmond place. Mrs. Richmond is all right but the bridge is out down there. He doesn't know when they can make it back."

Sharyn shook her head. "What about using the chopper?"

"I already thought of that. They said they can't go up in this weather."

"And the ambulance?"

"They called to ask if it was an emergency," Trudy explained. "They only have two rigs that can make it through the snow. They're both swamped with three heart attacks and a bad crash on the Interstate. They need us to hold on to Beau until they can get here."

"I know. Emergency priority rules," Sharyn replied. She was staring at Ernie. "And they're right. We'll hold him here until the ambulance or his wife can get here. Then we'll deal with it."

"What's up with Ernie?" Trudy wondered, following Sharyn's gaze to the water fountain where Ernie was standing.

"I don't know," Sharyn admitted. "Send David

over here to baby-sit Mr. Richmond until we can sort through all of this."

"Sure thing, Sheriff."

After seeing David installed in the conference room with Mr. Richmond, Sharyn took her place on the phones. Everything came through the office that night. From UFOs to people getting stuck in up-stairs windows as they tried to crawl out onto their roofs. The snow had begun to subside but the panic had just set in.

There were several new communities trapped by the bridge that was out by the Richmonds' place. There was another group of hikers caught in the snow on Diamond Mountain. The wreck on the Interstate was joined by another wreck on a back road going out of Diamond Springs. Some people just wanted to know the weather report or called be-cause they were scared.

Phone lines were out here and there. Sharyn con-sidered that it might be a blessing that they were. If there were any more people calling in, their phones might go down under the weight of the emergency usage.

Sharyn dispatched deputies where she thought they could help. They evacuated a small nursing home that had no power for the machines that kept their residents alive. Some motorists were stranded in their cars and deputies got them out and to a shelter.

Sharyn called her own home, like each of the deputies and Trudy. But Faye Howard was prepared for anything. She'd been married to a lawman for thirty years. There wasn't anything that could take her by surprise.

Caison, Sharyn noted wryly, was still there with her mother.

Sharyn put the thought from her mind. She didn't have time for anything but the situation at hand. Ed and Joe were still out, helping another stranded motorist. The county resource officer called and said that the plows were out on the roads, so they would see some relief that night. Until the roads froze again toward morning. Lennie and Mrs. Richmond had managed to be in the first group of people being taken out of the southeast area where the bridge went out. He had no ETA but at least they were on their way.

Nick and Jeremy, who were both sworn in as emergency deputies, joined the group in the sheriff's office. Sharyn was working on a plan to get the hikers off of Diamond Mountain. She glanced up and saw Nick's familiar scowl as he spoke on one of the phones. Jeremy was on a phone, too, but his face was composed and pleasant. Other county volunteers who were trained at emergency situations had trickled in, freeing the deputies who were handling emergencies out of the office.

"I'd like to go out," David told Sharyn a short

while later. "I've got my big four-wheel-drive truck. I could be doing some real good out there instead of baby-sitting that old man."

Sharyn looked up from the plan she was explaining with the chopper pilot. It had stopped snowing and he was going to fly up to the mountain and get those kids down.

"That old man is Beau Richmond," she explained. "Not to put too fine a point on it, David, but he helped us get the chopper and he's helped everyone in this town at one time or another."

"What about Ernie?" David demanded. "He's just skulking around somewhere. Why can't he sit with Richmond?"

"Because I need him to help handle emergencies that come through," she lied. She had no idea what Ernie was doing or if he was still there. She hadn't seen him in over an hour. There was a lost look about him that made her swallow the question she'd been about to ask him. "I need you to sit with Richmond, David. When his wife gets here or an ambulance gets through, then you can go out."

David frowned. "All right."

"How is he?" she wondered.

"He's sleeping with his head on the table, muttering a lot about killing some kid and ghosts getting him."

Sharyn nodded. "Okay. Just keep him company."

It was after midnight before things started slowing down. The snow had completely stopped, and while the roads were wet, they were becoming passable. Emergency teams had evacuated all the communities that were stranded by bridges being out. Storm shelters were overflowing, but at least they were tucked in for the night.

"Have you heard from Lennie?" Sharyn asked, wishing someone would get there and take Beau Richmond off her hands. It made her nervous to have him there.

"Not yet," Trudy answered. "Last time was about an hour ago."

The chopper pilot had reported in that the hiking group was safely off the mountain and in a shelter for the night. Plows had cleared most of the roads in and out of town and were starting on the outlying county areas. There was a water main break about a mile from the center of town but a crew had already been dispatched to take care of the problem.

Joe called in to let them know that one man had been killed in a wreck on the Interstate. All the rest of the injured had been dispatched to the hospital. He and Ed were staying to be sure nothing else happened until the wreck was cleared.

"Tell me that the ambulances are free now, Trudy," Sharyn requested.

Trudy yawned. "Haven't heard from them. Want me to call?"

"Yes." Sharyn looked around the crowded office. "Has anyone seen Ernie?"

"He was here just a minute ago," Nick growled his response. "Maybe he fell asleep under a desk."

"I'll check the restroom for him, Sheriff," Jeremy offered.

"Can't raise either ambulance right now, Sheriff," Trudy told her. "They're both in transit to the hospital."

"Remind me to be skiing next time it snows," Nick complained as he answered the phone. "Yeah, this is the emergency team. Whaddya want?" He looked at the phone in his hand. "They hung up."

"Imagine!" Trudy said as she walked by him.

"Has anyone made coffee in the last two hours?" Nick demanded with a significant glance at Trudy.

She smiled at him sweetly. "I don't know, Nick. Why don't you walk to the coffeepot and check it out?"

Nick put down his phone and did as Trudy suggested. Trudy winked at Sharyn and sat down at her desk.

Sharyn ignored everyone's odd moods and foul tempers. It was always like that during a crisis. The phone rang and she answered it. It was an elderly man who was wondering if the county plow could plow out his driveway for him to take his wife to the doctor the next day. She was in the process of explaining why they couldn't plow his driveway, when Assistant DA Michaelson walked through the front doors and shrugged out of his heavy coat.

"Who's in charge of this mess?" he demanded. "Where's the sheriff?"

Sharyn reassured the man on the phone one last time that they would find a way for him to get his wife to the hospital if it was an emergency, then she set down the phone.

Alan Michaelson had steadily become more aggressive as he spent more time in his position. He was in his mid-thirties, with brown hair and brown eyes. He was six feet of towering ambition and rampant ego. He was determined to make a name for himself in Diamond Springs, then make a stab at the state level. He was tough on crime and easy on guns. The district attorney, Jack Winter, had never come close to losing an election in twenty years, but Michaelson was biting at his coattails.

Sharyn wondered how his boss, the infamous Jack Winter, felt about his protégé trying to take his seat. It was rumored that men had disappeared for less. Most people were afraid of Jack Winter. She guessed Michaelson didn't have enough intelligence to take the other man seriously. It was between the two men, as far as she was concerned. But she didn't want Michaelson scoring points off of *her* office.

And that was becoming a problem which she took *very* seriously. If she ever found out how Michaelson got tipped off when things were happening at the office, she was going to fire whoever was responsible. It wasn't that the ADA and the sheriff's department didn't work together on every case. It was just that she didn't like the feeling that someone was sneaking around behind her back. It was part of her job to contact the DA's office. She didn't like to think that someone she trusted was one step ahead of her. And she didn't like people telling her how to do her job.

"Never mind," Michaelson told Trudy. "I see her." He walked to the desk where Sharyn was sitting with her phone. "So. Another homicide and we meet again, Sheriff."

"Michaelson."

"I know you're happy to see me but you're embarrassing me with your enthusiasm."

"What do you want, Michaelson?" she demanded.

He glanced around the office. "I hear you've already had a confession about that kid's bones you found at the training school. Nice work, Sheriff! I'm here to handle it for you."

"How did you hear that?" she wondered, sitting back in her chair and scrutinizing his face in the strange light.

Michaelson shrugged. "I have my sources. Where is he?"

"Who?"

"The suspect, Sheriff. Don't play games with me."

"Michaelson," she began. She saw the front door open and Lennie walk in with Mrs. Richmond. "Why don't you get some coffee?"

Michaelson leaned close to her. "Why don't you quit stalling?"

"When I'm ready to present a case to you, I'll call you," she told him finally. "You shouldn't have been out on a night like this."

"That's my job," he replied firmly.

"No," she answered, looking him straight in the eye. "Your job is to come when I'm ready to present a case. And you need to tell whoever called you with this, that when I find out who he or she is, they're history in this office."

Michaelson smiled nastily. "Threats, Sheriff?"

"Promises, Mr. Michaelson. Excuse me."

Sharyn met Lennie and Mrs. Richmond at the door. She escorted them quickly to her office and closed the door.

Julia Richmond was shaky and confused. "What's going on, Sheriff? Where's my husband?"

Lennie shook his head. "I didn't tell her the details."

"I'm sorry, Mrs. Richmond," Sharyn said quickly.

"Your husband is here but we hardly recognized him. He was incoherent when he came in. Then he confessed to a murder."

"A murder?" Julia demanded, horror written on her golden-girl good looks. "Who did he say he killed?"

"A young boy. He said he killed him forty years go."

Julia Richmond sat down hard in a chair. "I—I don't understand."

"Get her some coffee, Lennie, and don't let that leech Michaelson in here."

Lennie nodded and left them alone. Sharyn sat down beside Beau's wife. "I know this is hard but is there anything you can tell me about your husband's behavior the past few days?"

Julia shrugged. "I don't know. Where is he? Can I see him? I need to talk to him."

Sharyn tried again. "When was the last time you saw him?"

"He left the house just before the storm started. I looked for him but he didn't come back."

"When did you get home from the dinner?" Sharyn asked her.

"We left early, right after you, Sheriff, when we heard the weather was getting bad. Beau didn't want to be out in the storm."

"Was he acting strange before that?" Sharyn asked

her. "Did he mention anything to you about coming here?"

"No," Julia answered. "I don't understand why he'd come here."

"He didn't mention this crime to you?"

"No, not at all. Why would he say such a thing, Sheriff? You don't believe he killed anyone, do you?"

"I really don't know what to think," Sharyn told her truthfully. "He's obviously sincere but he also seems confused and distraught. I think he should go to the hospital. There might be a medical explanation for this."

"You think he's sick?"

"I think something is wrong, Mrs. Richmond. I'd hate for Mr. Richmond to be taken seriously on this murder if he's ill. Did you say anything to anyone else about this when the deputy came to get you?"

"Only Maria, the housekeeper. She won't mention it to anyone else."

"Okay," Sharyn decided. "Let's go and see your husband."

"He hasn't been arrested, has he, Sheriff?" Julia asked in a small voice.

"No, he hasn't," Sharyn told her. "That's why I want to keep this quiet."

Sharyn opened the door to her office. Michaelson and Nick were exchanging intent words over the new pot of coffee. She frowned. Was Nick her culprit?

Would he be willing to run to Michaelson with everything that happened?

Trudy was walking toward the interrogation room with a cup of fresh coffee and one of the doughnuts that had been brought in by the local bakery who'd donated them for the emergency. She knocked on the conference-room door. There was no response. She called David's name but the man didn't answer.

"I want you to talk with your husband, Mrs. Richmond," Sharyn told the woman. "We've called an ambulance for him."

"Is he hurt?" Julia asked in a pitiful voice. She looked at Lennie as he handed her a cup of coffee, then at Sharyn for support.

"No, at least I don't think so," Sharyn responded. "Although he might be having a stroke or something. He needs to be evaluated."

Trudy shrugged and walked to the side wall where they kept the key for the interrogation room. She juggled the doughnut and coffee and managed to open the heavy door, prepared to give David a piece of her mind for sleeping on the job.

"A stroke?" Julia Richmond questioned. "What makes you think he's having a stroke?"

Trudy's scream pierced the clamor and chaos of the office. It was followed immediately by the shattering of the coffee cup and the little plate she'd put the doughnut on as they crashed to the floor at her feet. For an instant, there was silence, then the room erupted into even more confusion.

"Trudy?" Sharyn ran to her side, reaching her as Nick and ADA Michaelson did. They crowded into the open doorway.

Trudy shook her head, wordlessly, and pointed to the far corner of the room. Julia Richmond screamed and collapsed on the floor beside Sharyn. Beau Richmond was hanging from the corner beam, a chair knocked over under his feet.

THREE

THE EERIE RED LIGHT made a strange picture of the
man's body hanging from the ceiling. Nick climbed
up on the conference table to reach Beau. Sharyn
was there beside him before he looked down to ask
for help.

"I'll lift him," he said.

Sharyn took out her pocketknife and nodded.

Beau's dead weight strained Nick's muscles as he
lifted the man to loosen the hold on his neck.

"I don't know why I stay in this business." Trudy
was fretting, wringing her hands. "People die all the
time. The hours are terrible. The pay is bad. You have
to see dead people who aren't even related to you!"

Sharyn heard Ernie soothing her, eventually leading her out of the room.

"What's going on?" David asked. "I only went to
the bathroom for a minute. What happened?"

Sharyn managed to cut through the leather that
was holding Beau swinging in the air. It looked like
his belt, although it was difficult to be certain in

the strange red emergency light. Lennie and David helped Nick lower Beau to the floor.

"Let me see that knife!" Nick yelled to Sharyn. He cut the leather from around Beau's throat when she'd given him the pocketknife. "Get the paramedics in here! We might still be able to help him!" He began giving Beau CPR while Lennie made the call to the ambulance.

"How long were you gone, David?" Sharyn demanded.

"Not long," David returned. "I went to the bathroom. I locked the door and told him I'd be back. He said he'd like another cup of coffee. He didn't sound frantic or anything. How was I supposed to know he'd do something like this?"

"Oh, Beau!" Julia Richmond screamed when she came to and saw her husband on the floor.

"Get her out of here," Sharyn said sharply.

"No, no! I want to see my husband!" the woman yelled and tried to push into the room.

"What's going on in here?" Michaelson wondered.

Sharyn got up and cleared the room. "Don't let anyone else in until the paramedics get here, David!"

"I have a right to be here with him," Julia cried hysterically. "I'm his wife! We belong together!"

"I'm sorry, Mrs. Richmond," Sharyn told her. "We'll do what we can for him."

David closed the door behind him, taking the grieving lady with him.

"Any luck?" Sharyn asked, taking her place at Nick's side again.

"I don't think so," Nick answered, drawing a breath. "I can't see anything in this light! How close is the ambulance?"

"I don't know. We've had trouble reaching them all night. They're on emergency rules right now. Priority cases only."

"I think this is a priority case," Nick told her. "Take over compressions. Don't forget to breathe."

Sharyn nodded, taking his place without missing a beat. Nick reexamined the man and shook his head. "There's no pulse, no breath activity."

"We can't just give up," Sharyn said.

"Even if we could bring him back at this point," he argued realistically, "he's probably brain dead."

The paramedics burst through the door at that moment. They took over from Nick and Sharyn, examining the man and calling it into the hospital. He was pronounced dead at a little after 1:00 a.m.

"No! He can't be dead!" his wife cried out. "Can't you do something else? Can't you shock him or open his chest like they do on television?"

The lead paramedic put his hand on Julia Richmond's arm. "I'm sorry, Mrs. Richmond. Beau meant the world to this whole town, but dead is dead, ma'am. I'm sorry."

They put Beau's body on a stretcher and covered it with a sheet, then they wheeled him out of the office. The power came back on around then, the city lighting up like thousands of lightning bugs in the dark night. Sharyn stood on the steps leading down to the street and shivered.

"Guess you were right, Sheriff," Michaelson said calmly. "There wasn't a suspect here."

Sharyn gritted her teeth but managed not to say anything as he walked back inside.

"Don't let him get to you," Lennie advised. "I'll have his job in a few years."

She smiled. "Thanks. I'd like to see that."

"Sheriff," Ernie said, stepping out of the office. "We're all exhausted. If we're not on duty, can we call it a night? I'd like to take Trudy home. She's in a state."

Sharyn turned and faced them. "No one is leaving here until we piece together what happened tonight. No matter what, we're going to be held responsible for Beau's death. He committed suicide in our conference room. I'm sure you all know that there's going to be repercussions. There has to be an investigation."

"But we weren't responsible for him killing himself," Trudy argued.

"He wasn't our prisoner but he was still our responsibility," she reminded them. "We have to be careful. The DA and the press are going to want someone's head. Are you volunteering yours, Trudy?"

Trudy shook her head. "No, ma'am."

"Then I think we all had better go back inside. I expect a report from each of you. Where you were, what you were doing in the last two hours. I'll interview you each separately."

"But David was responsible for Beau Richmond," Ernie pointed out. "Why all the rest of us?"

"Because we don't want to leave any stones unturned to surprise us. We do a thorough investigation now and hope for damage control. Michaelson has someone working in this office who's reporting to him. I don't know who it is. It could be one of you, for all I know."

They each demurred and assured her that none of them were working for Michaelson. Except Nick, who stood in stony silence.

"I'd like to do my report," Jeremy offered, "then I can go back to the morgue and get started on the autopsy. I assume there will be one?"

"Of course," Nick growled at him. "The man didn't exactly die at home in his bed surrounded by grieving relatives."

Jeremy nodded, his face serious as he looked to Sharyn. "I don't mind staying late to finish this up."

"All right," she agreed with a glance at Nick.

"I don't care," Nick added with graceless non-chalance. "Can we go inside now? It's freezing out here."

Sharyn sat in her own office, writing her report of where she saw each member of the group that night, retracing her own movements. Ed and Joe had finally made it back in and been met with pulling more time while the night deputies, Lennie and David, wrote their reports.

Sharyn appointed Ed and Joe to get the names and addresses of every volunteer who had been in the room that night. She heard the groaning but she shut her door on it.

How could this have happened? she wondered, taking a seat at her desk. And was there any way to save David's career? When the DA sorted through the facts, he was going to realize what Sharyn had already realized. David was lying. He had to be gone more than five minutes for Beau to have hanged himself.

Maybe she was the one to blame, she considered carefully. Maybe she should've assigned two people to look after Beau. She could see he was distraught but he seemed to calm down. He was lucid when he confessed to killing that boy. She didn't think he needed more than one person with him. But, honestly, in all of the emergency hoopla that was going on, she'd lost track of him.

Nick knocked on her door, then unceremoniously skidded his report across her desk. "Anything else? Maybe you'd like me to watch David while he fills out his report?"

"David's a good man," she defended. "He couldn't know Beau was suicidal."

David walked into the office behind Nick. He stared hard at Sharyn then put his report down on her desk. "My resignation is there with it."

She sighed. "Let's not go through this again, David. You don't have to resign."

"I was responsible. I left him alone. That's what they're all saying, isn't it?" He glared at Nick.

Nick yawned and looked away from him. "I'm going home. Since my assistant is handling the autopsy, I'm sure you'll have it before morning."

Sharyn nodded. "Thanks, Nick. I'm sure you've been helpful."

He raised his eyebrows, his dark eyes questioning. "Did you want me to perform the autopsy?"

"You *are* the medical examiner," she reminded him quietly. "There's going to be a lot of questions about this. I need to be sure."

"Are you saying you don't trust Jeremy?"

"I trust him," she replied. "I just think it wouldn't hurt to have your signature on the file with his."

Nick shrugged. "All right. I didn't need any sleep tonight anyway." He yawned again. "I'll call you when I'm done."

"Sit down, David," Sharyn invited the other man. "Close the door."

The phone rang as David closed the door. It was Jeremy from the morgue. "It was a simple hanging, Sheriff," he assured her. "Clear ligature marks; the leather had broken the skin."

"Was his neck broken?" Sharyn wondered.

"No. He suffocated."

"Thanks, Jeremy. Go home."

Jeremy laughed. "I will after I clean up here, Sheriff. It's been a long night, hasn't it?"

Sharyn agreed and hung up the phone. Her night wasn't likely to be over until everything was cleared up. Diamond Springs was still going to be in an uproar with the snow. There would still be more accidents on the roads, possibly even evacuations around the river once the snow started melting. All of her deputies were going to be exhausted.

David faced her across her desk. "I know we haven't always gotten along, Sheriff."

She nodded.

"But I appreciate what you said to Nick. Especially after we both know this was all my fault."

"Where were you?" she wondered.

He looked down at his shoes, fingers playing with his thick brown mustache. "I went outside in the lot for a while. The snow was still falling and it was so beautiful. I just wanted some fresh air."

"You drove your new truck," she gleaned from his statement. "How long?"

He shook his head. "Probably not more than thirty minutes, maybe an hour. No more. I left him, locked the door, put the key on the rack, then stepped outside with Charlie. You can ask him."

Sharyn tapped her pencil on her desk. "Thirty minutes to an hour?"

"On my honor, Sheriff." He crossed his heart.

She studied him closely. He always wore his brown hair too long for department regs. His uniform was rumpled from the long night and he had a coffee stain on his collar. Despite everything, she trusted David Matthews. Maybe he'd done something stupid, again, but she needed him. Especially right now.

"All right."

"Are you going to suspend me?"

"Not right now. I'd like for you to finish the night shift so Ed and Joe can go home and get some sleep for tomorrow."

"I can do that, Sheriff," David told her quickly, the gleam back in his brown eyes.

"Good. We'll fight this if Michaelson wants to give us a hard time. You *are* a good man, David. I depend on you."

He smiled. "Thanks. And you're a good sheriff, ma'am."

"Thanks. Take Joe's or Ed's place and send Lennie in, please."

"Sure."

Lennie came into her office and handed her his report. "David says you want me to take the rest of my shift?"

"That's right."

"If I might speak frankly, Sheriff?"

She put down her pencil and looked into his darkly handsome face. "Go ahead."

"You aren't going to come up looking good on this one, Sharyn. You need to establish that it was Matthew's fault and get rid of him."

"I don't work like that, Lennie, but thanks for your advice."

He shrugged. "I know what I'd see if I were looking at this the way Michaelson will look at it."

"How's that?"

"Deputy Matthews was responsible for the prisoner and he left him. Mr. Richmond committed suicide because of it. It was clear negligence."

Sharyn placed his report in a folder. "Don't worry, Lennie. I'll handle Michaelson."

Lennie smiled. He was once voted the sexiest player in the NFL, and his smile was named one of his best features. "I'd just hate to lose you, Sharyn."

"Thanks, Lennie." She smiled in return. "I'm not going anywhere."

Ernie came in with his statement and Trudy's. "She fell asleep on the sofa. Can I take her home?"

"In a minute," Sharyn told him. "Ernie, Jeremy says that Beau suffocated after he hanged himself. His neck wasn't broken. David swears that he wasn't outside for more than thirty minutes to an hour. Does that seem odd to you?"

Ernie shrugged and for once his lucid brown eyes didn't meet hers. "I don't know, Sheriff. I'm too tired to think. Maybe we can talk about this tomorrow?"

She nodded. "Sure, Ernie. Go ahead, take Trudy home. She's had enough for one day."

Ernie closed the door to Sharyn's office and stood outside for a long moment. He put his hand on the heavy door panel and closed his eyes. Then he turned away and went to get Trudy.

All the reports were turned in and the list of volunteers was alphabetized. Sharyn looked over the reports and put them together in their order of importance. She looked up at the pictures of her father and grandfather, scowling down at her from the wall.

David had made a mistake. A mistake that might cost him his career. She thought she could see the out on it but she wasn't sure. The DA would be investigating them and he would come down hard. After all, it *was* Beau Richmond. Either Winter or Michaelson were going to be playing to the press. Either one would be looking for a head.

Sharyn was pretty sure that Michaelson would like it to be hers. She was playing into his hands by supporting David, but it just wasn't her way to leave a man hanging out to dry.

She yawned and looked at her computer screen again. Besides, something was wrong. Instinct told her that but her brain was too tired to function. She rubbed her eyes and wished she could talk to Ernie. She wished she knew what was wrong with Ernie. Lennie was dazzling and ambitious but she'd trade a day with him for five minutes with Ernie.

Ernie's father had died right after Annie's father, Delbert Anderson. Somehow it had created a strange union between them. Their grief, and the investigation into town hero Billy Bost's death, brought them back together.

Sharyn didn't know the whole story but she did know that Annie and Ernie had been sweethearts in high school. She'd married another man and had a daughter, but she'd left him after meeting Ernie again. They'd been together ever since.

It was a lot to deal with emotionally. Sharyn understood that and she'd looked the other way for the past few months while Ernie was late for duty and left early. It strained their friendship and their working relationship. It wasn't that Ernie was just obsessed with finally finding Annie again. It was something more.

But at that moment, she was too tired to try to figure it out. She'd thought about it a lot but decided again and again to wait for him to find himself. Ernie meant too much to her to think about losing him. He had to snap out of it.

It was about 8:30 when Nick wandered back into the sheriff's office. He'd tried to call her a few times from the morgue but there was no answer. Trudy was off, after her unpleasant experience, and the temp was a surly woman who had refused to walk into Sharyn's office to see if she was there. He'd called her house and Faye had told him that she'd never come home after the storm.

Glaring at the temp, who was polishing her nails and reading a magazine, Nick stormed into Sharyn's office, only to find her asleep at her computer. She was making a little whistling sound when she breathed and her tousled red curls were spilling over her arm where she'd laid her head. He put one hand on her arm to shake her but left it too long.

She blinked up at him like a startled bird. "Nick?"

He quickly withdrew his hand. "You look awful."

"Thanks." She pulled herself upright and yawned. "What time is it?"

"About eight forty-five," he answered.

"Okay." She yawned again and shook her head. "What time is it?"

"About eight forty-six," he said with a small smile playing over his face. "Come on, Sharyn. Wash your face and I'll buy you breakfast."

Sharyn walked like a zombie into the ladies' room. She washed her face and looked at her puffy red eyes and wrinkled uniform. She brushed her hair and did what she could with the rest of her appearance. Leave it to Nick to wake her up after two hours' sleep.

She was surprised to find herself at the small diner down the street, a cup of coffee in front of her. Nick ordered for both of them, then sat back and watched her sip her coffee.

"So?" she asked finally, nervously aware of him staring at her. "I know you aren't up and dragging me around for nothing. What did you find?"

"What did Jeremy find?"

She shrugged. "Nick, I'm not playing games with you this morning."

He sat forward. "I could've called and had you come down to the morgue. We could've looked at Beau Richmond's body together."

She sighed. "Jeremy called right after you left last night and told me that Beau had suffocated. His neck wasn't broken."

Nick sipped his coffee. "Think again."

The waitress put down their food and poured them more coffee. Sharyn looked at the eggs and toast on her plate and drank more coffee.

"Beau was murdered."

"What?"

"Beau was murdered. Right there in the conference room of the sheriff's office."

Sharyn stared at him. "How? Did someone put a pillow over his head?"

He smiled. "Jeremy is good but he was looking to confirm the obvious theory. I found blunt trauma to the back of Beau's head. Whoever hit him, hit him hard. He wasn't dead before they hanged him but the two combined made it faster."

Sharyn snapped her fingers. "That's it! David said he was gone for less than an hour. I knew it would've taken Beau longer to suffocate. What kind of weapon?"

"Something like the butt of a gun or a police nightstick."

"Either thing was easy to find there last night."

"Exactly," he answered, looking satisfied.

"Don't look so smug," she told him angrily. "This

makes everyone here last night a suspect, including you."

Nick raised a coal-black brow. "Why would *I* kill him?"

"Why would anyone there kill him?"

"You have as much reason as I do."

"Maybe," she replied, looking smug herself. "But I'm the sheriff. Did you know Beau Richmond, Nick?"

"We didn't exactly travel in the same circles," he said flatly. "Are you accusing *me?*"

"That's my job, Nick. I ask questions. People explain."

"The closest I came to him before last night was at a blood drive at the television station three years ago. We were next to each other giving blood. Happy?"

Sharyn sipped coffee. "Have you been seeing his wife?"

"What?"

She played with her coffee cup and saucer. "Well, whoever you see in your personal life you keep pretty quiet," she continued logically. "Is she married?"

Nick smiled demonically and sat back in his seat. "Are you asking me if I'm seeing anyone, Sharyn?"

"I'm asking you if you're seeing Julia Richmond, Nick." She refused to be flustered by his devil-black eyes.

"No, Sheriff," he replied smoothly, buttering a

slice of toast. "There's only one woman in my life. She takes up all of my time. Besides, Julia Richmond isn't my type."

"Oh?" Sharyn wondered, pushing her luck.

Nick flashed her a smile that would have put him on equal part with Lennie Albert. "She's not a redhead."

Sharyn choked on her sip of coffee and signaled the waitress. "Could I get this to go?" The woman nodded and Sharyn swallowed the last of her coffee. "Thanks for breakfast, Nick. I better get on this before Michaelson hears about it."

Nick bit off a piece of toast, feeling pleased with himself. "Sure."

Sharyn picked up her hat and looked at him closely. "You aren't the one feeding Michaelson information, are you?"

Nick's face turned serious. "Not if he cut off my toes."

She smiled and took her boxed breakfast from the waitress. "Thanks, Nick."

"Call me if you need me, Sharyn."

"I will."

When she reached the office, Ed and Joe had come in for the day shift. Ernie was there and Lennie was still doing paperwork from the night before. She took them all into her office and explained Nick's findings.

"That's what was bothering me when I heard

that Beau had suffocated from the noose around his neck," she told them. "There wasn't enough time."

"If you can believe anything David says," Joe added with an apologetic look at Ed.

"David's an idiot sometimes," Ed defended his sister's son. "But he's not a liar."

"I think he said he only went to the bathroom," Joe told him.

"He came clean right after with the sheriff. No one knew this was gonna happen," Ed reminded his partner.

"So you think the sheriff should take the fire for him?"

"Slow down," Sharyn intervened. "No one's taking any fire yet. No one knows about this yet, except for us and Nick. I want to get everyone else out of the office and search everything thoroughly. It's possible the weapon is still here."

"Who would want to kill Beau Richmond?" Lennie asked. "The man was a saint. Everyone loved him."

Sharyn frowned. "Apparently not." She looked at Ernie, who'd remained silent. "All right. Let's give the temp—"

"Martha," Ed supplied with a quick smile.

Joe laughed and nudged his partner.

"Let's give *Martha* a break. Is there anyone else here?"

"A deputy from Allen County looking into that accident on the county line last night," Lennie added quickly.

"Okay. Let's get him out, too, for a while. We'll divide up and take a close look around."

"Shouldn't we be checking our own guns and nightsticks for hair and skin samples from Mr. Richmond?" Lennie suggested.

Everyone else looked at him.

"We are technically suspects," he assured them. "All of us. Michaelson will make that clear when he gets here."

Sharyn winced. "He's right. Everyone turn in your guns and nightsticks. We're going to be investigating ourselves."

"Anyone could've had access to that key David put on the wall," Joe said, resenting the idea that he was a murder suspect. "Anyone could've come in from outside."

"You and Ed are the only ones who have an alibi," Sharyn reminded him. "Both of you were out on the highway."

"What about the volunteers who were here last night?" Lennie questioned.

"We'll have to bring them all in," Sharyn acknowledged. "But let's do this first."

They all filed out of Sharyn's office. Ed went to break the news to Martha while he made plans to meet her for lunch. Lennie told the Allen County deputy that he could get coffee down the street and they would come for him.

"Sharyn," Ernie began when it was only the two of them in her office.

"What is it, Ernie?"

He started to speak but thought better of it. "My gun and nightstick are at home. I—I left them there this morning."

Sharyn looked into his eyes and didn't like what she saw there. "What is it really, Ernie?"

"What do you mean?"

"I mean, what's wrong with you, Ernie? You left your gun and nightstick at home? Last night you couldn't help with Beau. You walk around here like some kind of ghost. I know it's been rough the last few months, Ernie—"

"You have no idea," he assured her, his voice trembling slightly with his emotions. "You don't understand."

"Tell me, then!" she invited. "I want to help, Ernie—"

"You can't help, Sheriff," he said plainly. "I'm going to get my gun and nightstick."

"Ernie—"

"You can't help everyone, Sheriff," he told her. "I'll be back later."

Sharyn watched him leave, wondering what devils

he could be facing to make him act this way. Ernie was nothing if not solid and dependable. Hadn't her father always trusted him when he was sheriff? Hadn't she done the same in the two years she'd been sheriff? Ernie had never let her down. She didn't think he was letting her down now, but she wished she could have his help on this case.

When Martha had been charmed out of her seat at the switchboard and the deputy from Allen County had left the building, muttering about crazy people, the deputies split up into pairs. Sharyn didn't want anyone going alone. Whatever they found, they found together, so that Michaelson couldn't question the validity or the motive behind the find.

That, of course, was saying the weapon was still in the building. Since they didn't see anyone sashay in and out of the conference room, how unlikely was it that the person just took the weapon with him?

"We have to have forensics go over this room," Lennie reminded her bluntly when they started in the conference room.

"I know," she agreed, handing him a pair of latex gloves.

The fluorescent light above them glitched a little, causing a wave effect on the walls and floor. There was very little place in that room to hide anything like a gun or a nightstick.

Sharyn checked the duct coming into the room.

The killer had been near the ceiling when he was hanging Beau's body with his belt. But there was nothing there. She opened the windows and looked down at the ground but the snow made an easy job of finding anything. Nothing but white crystal lay on the ground outside the window.

"Ed and Joe are lucky they weren't here last night," Lennie said, feeling under the table with his hand. "At least they aren't suspects."

"Anyone who has a key or had access to the key to this room is a suspect," Sharyn reminded him. "That makes a lot of people. Ed and Joe are lucky that they have an alibi for that time because they were both out at the wreck site. Otherwise they still wouldn't be in the clear."

"Of course, not everyone is going to have a motive," Lennie continued, thinking out loud. "In fact, most of the people here last night didn't even know Beau."

"That's true," Sharyn admitted, getting down from the table. "But someone knew him and had a reason to want him dead. I hate to do it but we're going to have to talk to Julia today. Beau was well liked around here but he was also a wealthy, powerful businessman. I'm sure he had his share of enemies."

"Who sneaked in here last night, took the key, and hit him on the head, then strung him up?"

She took a deep breath. "Something like that."

"There's nothing under the table," Lennie announced, sitting down heavily on the floor. "I don't see anyplace else to hide anything in this room."

"I don't either," Sharyn said. "Let's seal the room for forensics and look in the office."

"Are we searching your office, Sheriff?" Lennie wondered, dark eyes focusing on her freckled face.

"Of course," she told him. "I'm not having Michaelson say we left anyone or anything out of the search."

"What about Ernie?"

"What about him?"

"He left right away. Why isn't he involved? He was here last night."

"That's between me and Ernie," Sharyn pointed out coolly.

Lennie shrugged broad shoulders. "Okay. But that's where I'd look. You said he's been acting weird. Everybody's noticed it. Then he leaves today while we're searching the office."

"Yeah, well, let's finish the search and conjecture later," Sharyn said, unwilling to discuss Ernie with Lennie.

But there was some grain of truth in his statement. Certainly there was enough that Michaelson could see it. Ernie was acting strangely. He had left his gun and nightstick at his house. He was there last night, and he and Beau actually knew each other. She hadn't asked him about it but it sounded as though they'd grown up together.

It was ridiculous, but she had to consider what it was going to look like to the DA. What she thought about Ernie and what Michaelson thought were two different things.

"Well, lookie here," Lennie said as he started to get up from the floor. He looked into the gray trash can and pulled out some papers with his gloved hand. "It looks like Beau had enough time to write a little confession."

"What?"

Sharyn looked at the piece of paper, actually the back of a yellow legal pad with doodles on it from another meeting in the conference room earlier in the day. They had been plotting their strategy for emergency routes in case of snow that night. Sharyn recognized Ed's pretty girl faces.

I was sixteen when I was picked up and put into Jefferson Training School. I latched on to Walt right away and together, we started picking on the smaller kids, especially Michael Smith. He never fit in, never had friends. He was strange and different from the rest of us. We were both sixteen when we led Michael down that embankment by the bridge, hit him in the back of

the head, and rolled him down into the ditch.
When we saw that he was dead, we buried him.
God have mercy on my soul and my friend
Walter Hamilton. God save us both.

She handed the paper to Lennie for him to read.

"Couldn't ask for a better confession of the crime," Lennie decided.

"Walter Hamilton," Sharyn whispered. "Judge Walter Hamilton?"

Lennie shivered. "I hope not. That man makes me want to go and clean my room or something. He just has that look.

She smiled. "He looks like that picture of George Washington on his chamber wall."

"Yeah." Lennie looked at her. "Do you think it could be the same guy?"

"There's only one way to tell," she realized. "Back then, the juvenile records weren't sealed. Jefferson was proud of its achievements. There was a yearbook put together for the boys. I've seen a few of them."

"Think we can find one going back that far?"

"I don't know. We'll have to look through the school records to be sure. I'll have Ernie do that when he gets back."

"What about this?" He held out the yellow paper.

"We keep this between us until we can find out if it's the same man," she decided.

They walked out into the office and ADA Michaelson was waiting for them.

"Find something interesting, Sheriff?"

FOUR

"So, Beau Richmond was murdered," Michaelson stated.

"As if we didn't know *that* already," Joe quipped quietly.

"Did you have something to say, Deputy?" the attorney asked.

"No, sir."

"Good. It's obvious to me that the sheriff's office can't police themselves in this matter. I have full authority from the district attorney to set up an investigation. You'll report directly to me. Everyone in the county is going to want to know that Mr. Richmond's death was properly investigated, without any impropriety by this office."

Ernie chose that moment to walk through the front doors to the office holding his gun and nightstick.

"What's going on here?" Michaelson questioned. "Are these the murder weapons?"

"No, sir," Ernie replied. "I left my gun and nightstick at home this morning. I wasn't on duty last night so I didn't have them with me."

Michaelson swiveled and smiled at Sharyn. "In your office, Sheriff, please."

Sharyn followed in Michaelson's wake and closed the door while he took the seat behind her desk. Things were going from bad to worse that day, and her head was starting to ache.

"Sheriff, do you have any excuse for this?"

"This?" she queried.

"Tampering with evidence."

"Ernie's gun and nightstick aren't evidence. I had all the deputies bring in their guns and nightsticks to be checked."

"Because you thought one of them could be the murder weapon and you were moving quickly to cover up for the man?"

Sharyn stared him down. "I wouldn't cover up a murder for any man here today, including you, Michaelson! But I do want to find the truth. I told you before, I don't play political games. That's not part of my job."

He laughed. "You have no hope for reelection, Sheriff."

She shook her head. "Sometimes that doesn't strike me as a bad thing."

"Well, we're going to do this investigation my way, Sheriff. Right down the middle. I'm going to be watching every move you make until we find out who killed Beau Richmond. I tried to convince the district attorney to have you removed from this case. After all, you're a suspect, too. But Mr. Winter wouldn't hear of it. He likes you, Sheriff."

"Then on whose authority are you here?" she demanded, ready to kick him out of her office.

"Oh, he believes I should oversee the investigation," Michaelson hastened to assure her. "He just thinks you should do the investigating."

Sharyn had only met the DA, Jack Winter, twice. Once at her father's funeral and another time at a political function. They were both on the same party ticket. Otherwise, he was a reclusive man who sent his hired gun out to do his dirty work. And to take the heat if he was wrong.

"In that case—"

"In that case," Michaelson finished, "I've called the medical examiner and his assistant over to report their findings to your deputies. They'll be collecting the guns and nightsticks as well as doing the forensic work in the office."

Sharyn leaned on the desk and glared at him. "I won't work this way, Michaelson! Either you back off and let us do our jobs, or I'm not in this investigation."

"That's fine with me, Sheriff. If you choose to leave, I'm sure we can arrange some vacation time for you."

Sharyn knew he was calling her bluff. The problem was, she *was* bluffing. She didn't want Michaelson conducting any investigation that might involve Ernie, without her being there. If there was a problem, she wanted to know about it before Michaelson.

And she needed the time to look into her own thoughts about Ernie's recent behavior and his behavior last night. She knew how easily an investigation could go astray, and the wrong man could be charged with the crime. Hadn't that happened to her own father? She had set the matter right before the wrong man had been executed for the crime, but the mistake was made.

Nick came charging into her office and faced the two of them staring angrily at each other. He took one look at Sharyn's face and knew what she was thinking. *"You aren't the one feeding Michaelson information, are you?"*

"Dr. Thomopolis," Michaelson greeted him respectfully. "I'm glad you're here. I'd like you and your assistant to confiscate every gun and nightstick here. The sheriff is included in that request."

Sharyn didn't speak. Her mouth was drawn in a mutinous line but she handed her gun to Nick and left the room. She gathered her deputies together while the forensics team began working in the room. "We're going to have to cooperate with this idiot."

"Aw, Sheriff," Ed argued, taking out his gun to give it to Jeremy. "Can't we just shoot him?"

Sharyn smiled. "They'd just hire another one."

Joe laughed. "They'd get sick of it after a while. Or nobody would take the job."

"All right," she agreed darkly. "I'd like to tell them where to get off, too, but we can't right now. Let me just say one thing—*we* work together on this, no matter what *he* says. You come to me with whatever you find and we'll decide where to go from there. Be careful with your radios. Don't say too much."

"If your huddle is finished," Michaelson interrupted them, "maybe we can find Beau Richmond's murderer."

"The room was pretty clean," one of Nick's forensic students told them as they walked through the office. "Except for the table. We collected what we could find there but there were hundreds of prints! Should we head back and check them against the deputies' prints?"

Nick nodded. "Yeah, do that, Tommy, thanks. I'll be back when we're done here."

They sat around the old wooden table, scarred by fights and Cokes and boots. More than one of them looked up at the ceiling where Beau had been hanging. Sharyn saw Ed doodling his pretty girl faces and frowned. She still had Beau Richmond's last message in her pocket. Michaelson hadn't seen it yet. She was withholding evidence. She saw Lennie glance her way but he nodded grimly. She knew he wouldn't say anything unless she told him it was all right.

"Dr. Thomopolis, if you'd like to share your findings with us," Michaelson invited.

"Doctor?" Joe whistled. "Nick, are you a doctor?"

"He did cure my gout last spring," Ed supplied.

"The man is a professor, smarter than all of you put together," Michaelson told them bluntly. "He deserves some respect."

Ed snickered and Joe made faces behind Michaelson's back.

"Anyway," Nick went on with it, "Beau Richmond was killed by a blow to the back of the head. I'd say it came up with force, someone slightly shorter than him but since he was a tall man, that doesn't let anyone here off. There was no glass or wood or metal in the wound, so it was inflicted by something smooth and rounded."

"A nightstick or a gun butt," Ernie supplied softly.

"Exactly," Nick agreed. "Although we're not restricted to those weapons. He was hit with great force, and of course, he was lifted to the ceiling and hanged. Our killer was pretty strong."

"Guess that lets you off," Joe teased Ed.

"We weren't here, idiot!"

"That's right," Michaelson agreed. "I haven't had time to look through all of your statements yet. I'm sure the sheriff will give them to me when we're done here. But until we check out the other stories, you two will be in charge of this investigation."

Ed and Joe both looked at Sharyn.

Michaelson grimaced. Sharyn Howard's deputies were fanatically loyal. Not that he cared. They didn't have to like him, just do what he told them. "I'm in charge of this investigation. Since nearly the whole office could be considered suspects, I'll be making the decisions."

Sharyn still didn't say anything. Nick looked at her but she didn't look up at him. *Why didn't she say something?*

"Oh, I get it," Joe said, nudging Ed with his elbow.

Ed smiled. "Oh, yeah."

Lennie nodded and glanced at Ernie.

Ernie frowned but nodded his head as well.

Michaelson gritted his teeth. Something was already going on behind his back and he'd only been there an hour! "Do you have something you want to say, Sheriff?"

"No, sir," Sharyn replied briskly. "You're in charge."

"Good." Michaelson was happy with that admission.

Nick frowned. Whatever was going on, he hadn't been included. Again.

Jeremy walked into the room and gave each of the deputies a voucher for their gun and nightstick.

He gave the last one to the sheriff then took a seat at the table.

"So, where do we start?" Michaelson asked in general.

There was no response.

"You're only making this harder on yourselves," the ADA told them. "You could all be suspended without pay until your names are cleared."

Joe shrugged. "I was thinking about doing some fishing."

"Yeah," Ed responded. "I heard they're biting down by the dam."

"Not you two!" Michaelson reprimanded. "You're not suspected of anything."

"Oh." Ed smiled. "Sorry."

"Where do you usually start investigating a case like this?" Michaelson demanded.

Ernie cleared his throat and held up his hand until the ADA called on him. "Usually the head of the investigation decides where to start, sir."

Michaelson grimaced. "And that would be?"

"The sheriff, sir," Ernie supplied.

David chose that moment to walk into the conference room and slam the door behind him. "If you're all sitting around trying to decide how to frame me for this murder, I at least want my say!"

"No one's framing you for anything," Sharyn assured him. "Sit down, David."

"Well, since you brought it up—" Michaelson pounced on David's suggestion "—did you know Beau Richmond?"

"Only by reputation," David replied tensely. "I'd never met him before last night."

"What about his wife?" Nick asked and was rewarded with a withering look from Sharyn.

"I never saw his wife before, except in the papers."

"Then why would you kill him?" Michaelson demanded.

"I didn't kill him!"

"Did you leave the room to help someone else kill him? Who paid you to leave the room?"

Sharyn stood up. "No one paid him to leave the room," she defended her deputy. "It was a case of doing something without thinking about the consequences. David didn't know either one of the Richmonds. He didn't have any reason to kill Mr. Richmond. Surely even you must be able to see this was a spontaneous act? No one could have planned for Beau Richmond to be here. All he could do was take advantage of the situation once he was."

Michaelson studied her face thoughtfully. "If that's the case, Sheriff, then where do we start looking for our killer?"

Sharyn removed the piece of yellow notepad from her pocket and tossed it on the table. "I'd suggest we start here, Mr. ADA."

Michaelson read the paper quickly and his ruddy face blanched. "I know you're not suggesting we go after a district court judge for this?"

Trudy knocked then entered the room. "Sheriff, four-car pileup on the Interstate just out of town, and they're having trouble at the YMCA shelter."

"Thanks, Trudy," Sharyn said with a smile. "I'm glad to see you changed your mind."

She shrugged. "What good does it do to stay at home and think about it? I can't un-see it! Besides, that girl was getting jelly doughnut all over my desk!"

Everyone laughed, except Ed, who bemoaned losing Martha.

"She was too young for you anyway," Trudy told him bluntly.

"I think we should settle down," Michaelson interjected.

"Ed and Joe, take the pileup," Sharyn instructed naturally. "Ernie, check out the YMCA. Take Lennie with you."

"I'm not on duty," Lennie complained.

"You're here," Sharyn replied. "The next few days, everybody's going to have to sleep in shifts."

"Until we find the killer?" Lennie asked.

"No, until the snow melts. Be careful you're not one of the statistics from this blizzard."

Without another thought, most of the deputies filed out of the conference room and left the building.

Michaelson was blazing. "I'm in charge of this investigation."

"You're not in charge of this department," Sharyn answered him quickly. "This investigation is going to take place but everything else has to run smoothly, too. We do more around here than just investigate murders."

"This investigation is supposed to take priority," Michaelson repeated to her.

Sharyn locked gazes with him. "This is my department. You might be overseeing this investigation but I'll run this office the way I see fit. The DA can try to find a judge to suspend me but until that happens, I'm the sheriff."

Michaelson was speechless.

Nick smirked and gathered his papers together. "We're going back to take a look at everything we got today," he told the ADA. "Jeremy?"

Jeremy nodded and left the room behind Nick without a word.

"What about the investigation?" Michaelson asked.

"Well, David and I are going to see Julia Richmond this morning. If you don't want us to question Judge Hamilton until we have more proof, I think that's the best place to start."

"I'm late for court—" Michaelson nodded, consulting his watch "—or I'd go with you. But I want to see the report on that visit!"

Sharyn smiled. "That's fine."

David grinned at Sharyn's retreating back as she left the room before him. "She's a pistol, isn't she?"

Michaelson shuddered. "Among other things."

David ran out after Sharyn, grabbing his jacket as he left. "Thanks, Sheriff."

"For what?" she wondered as she put on her sunglasses against the bright sun glinting on the snow.

"Standing up for me," he answered, catching up with her. "I know you're taking me with you on this to show everybody that you have confidence in me."

Sharyn unlocked her car door and shook her head. "That's a lot to read into making you work when you're off duty."

"You're tricky, Sheriff," he told her as he climbed into her Jeep beside her. "But you're okay."

"Thanks," she said, starting the cold engine. "I'll remind you of that next time we disagree."

He laughed. "You know, you should really have an assistant sheriff who could take over for you when you're sick or on vacation. A formal assistant."

Sharyn nodded, negotiating the large piles of melting snow that had been thrown on the side of the street by the plows. "Formal assistant?"

"Yeah," David speculated. "He'd be in charge

when you couldn't be. He'd make more money and have a little metal ID that said he was the assistant sheriff."

Sharyn laughed. "First of all, you know the commissioners wouldn't let me pay anybody an extra dime right now. And second, you're all deputy sheriffs. That's what that means."

David shrugged. "But this deputy would be in charge of telling the other deputies what to do when you weren't here."

Sharyn glanced at him but kept herself from laughing at his transparent bid for status. "I'll have to talk to Ernie about it."

"Ernie?"

"He's been here the longest," she reminded him.

"But I've been with the department longer than you!"

"But I won the election." She pulled the Jeep into the Richmonds' drive. "Simple, huh?"

Sharyn spoke to the Richmonds' gatekeeper and showed him her badge. The man buzzed them through the electric gate. The long drive was elegant and carefully manicured. Piles of snow obscured some bushes and topped small trees but the pavement was clear and dry.

When the house appeared, David's mouth dropped open. "Wow!"

Sharyn looked at the Tudor-style mansion and shrugged. "It's big all right."

"Big? It's gorgeous!"

Sharyn pulled the Jeep up to the front of the circular drive. A man in a dark business suit answered the door and showed them into the house. The foyer was richly appointed with tapestries, artwork, and gleaming wood. The carpet underfoot made any sound impossible. An immense crystal chandelier hung from the thirty-foot peak above them.

"I'll get Mrs. Richmond," the man said in solid undertones.

Sharyn wondered if his somber, quiet tones were in deference to his employer's death or if Beau just liked a quiet house. Certainly, his lack of children in five marriages pointed toward the latter.

"I bet this stuff is real," David said, looking around at the priceless antiques and artwork.

Before Sharyn could answer, Julia Richmond sailed into the room in flowing black lace and chiffon, wafting Chanel perfume. "Good morning, Sheriff." She smiled at David and extended her hand. "Deputy. I'm glad I'm able to thank you for your... help last night."

Sharyn thought David was either going to kiss her hand or bow to her. She forestalled either action by telling Julia how deeply sorry they were for her husband's loss.

Julia smiled shakily and took a seat on the brocade sofa. "Thank you, Sheriff. Beau was a great man."

"He was," Sharyn agreed. "I hate to bring you this news and add to your misery, Mrs. Richmond, but we've discovered that Beau was killed."

"Killed?"

"Murdered. In the sheriff's office."

"What? How is that possible?"

"We're not sure yet, ma'am," David answered. "We're investigating."

Julia took out a dainty white handkerchief and dabbed at her nose. "I just can't believe it. Who would want to kill Beau? Everyone loved Beau!"

"Someone didn't, Mrs. Richmond." Sharyn had to set the record straight. "We need to try to get some ideas from you on where to start to look for that person."

Julia shrugged elegantly. "I just don't know, Sheriff."

"What about his ex-wives?" Sharyn suggested.

"I'll be glad to give you their names and numbers, Sheriff," Julia replied. "But they all loved Beau. He was very generous with them."

Sharyn frowned. "What about business associates?"

"Beau was well thought of, as far as I know, Sheriff," Julia told her. "I'll certainly allow you to look through his things but I can't imagine Beau having an enemy. Even his competitors thought well of him."

Sharyn hesitated. "Did you know that your husband was in a training school when he was sixteen for stealing cigarettes and skipping school?"

Julia blinked her eyes. "I had no idea! Beau stole something?"

"When he was a child," Sharyn said calmly. It didn't surprise her that it wasn't common knowledge. "He confessed to committing a crime while he was at the school."

"The murder you told me about last night?"

"He said he killed a boy," David filled in the gap. "He said ghosts and demons were visiting him because he killed that boy and that he couldn't rest."

Julia furrowed her pretty brow. "Sheriff, I can't say that I didn't know something was wrong with Beau for the past few months. He didn't speak to me about what was wrong. He surely didn't mention killing anyone."

"What made you think something was wrong, Mrs. Richmond?" Sharyn asked.

"Beau was…restless. It wasn't like him. He didn't sleep and couldn't eat. He didn't go to work. I tried to talk to him but he didn't want to talk about what was wrong. I tried to get him to see a doctor but he refused."

Sharyn studied Julia Richmond. Her dark, silky

hair was coiled like a coronet on her dainty head. She was probably about twenty-three, younger than Sharyn, yet married to a man twice her age. She wore expensive jewelry and her hands were carefully manicured. Her dark eyes weren't red with weeping for her recently dead husband but she was very pale. Sharyn recalled how lively and stunning she had been at the fund-raiser.

She would have asked the lovely young widow the obvious question but she and Lennie had been stuck, trying to cross the bridge, at about the same time her husband had been murdered.

"Did you notice anything that preceded Mr. Richmond's change in attitude?"

Julia considered the question. "Now that you mention it, he canceled a meeting and went to see Walt."

Sharyn looked up from her notepad. "Walter Hamilton?"

"That's right. He called this morning when he learned about Beau. He was very disturbed."

"Do you know what he talked to Judge Hamilton about, Mrs. Richmond?"

Julia shrugged. "I'm afraid I don't. I thought it was a business meeting. It was unusual for Beau to cancel things, that's why I remember it so well. He went to see Judge Hamilton, then he was different when he came home that night. He was never himself again."

Sharyn closed her notebook. "I would like to look at your husband's office, if I could," she told Julia.

"Of course. Follow me."

Julia led them to a huge study with shelves of books and comfortable chairs that faced a big desk. The whole room looked out over the tennis courts behind the mansion.

"I'm going to go and dress, if that's all right," Julia told them sweetly.

"Of course," David jumped in to assure her. "Take your time."

When they were alone in Beau Richmond's office, Sharyn began to look carefully through the dead man's property.

David stood at the door and watched Julia Richmond walk away. "Did you see the way she looked at me?"

"David—"

"I know she noticed me."

"David—"

"She is one fine-looking woman, Sheriff."

"David!"

He turned back. "Oh, sorry. What do you want me to do?"

Sharyn had him look through the files for anything that pertained to Judge Hamilton but there was nothing. She looked through Beau's desk, surprised to find that his appointment calendar was empty after yesterday. It was as though he'd known for a while what he was going to do and had purposely stopped working. His calendar was filled with appointments prior to that day.

Maybe he would have committed suicide anyway, she speculated, but someone beat him to it. Someone who didn't want to wait for him to tell his story. Judge Hamilton? It was beginning to look that way. She glanced back at the appointment days when Beau had Walter Hamilton on his calendar. It had been about two months ago when they'd had their first meeting, then they'd met again about two weeks ago.

Something nibbled at the back of Sharyn's awareness. It was Ernie. He'd been strange for about the same amount of time. She knew he wasn't involved in anything that Beau Richmond and Walter Hamilton had going on together. It was probably coincidence. Unfortunately, Sharyn didn't believe in coincidence. She was going to have to talk to Ernie.

"Hey, look at this," David said, pulling something out of the file cabinet.

It was an old photo of a large group of boys of varying ages with Jefferson Training School's solid image in the background. The picture was old. The bridge to the chapel was there but only partially built. Sharyn looked at the grainy black-and-white photo but she couldn't tell Judge Hamilton or Beau Richmond from all of the other boys. One of the boys, a smallish young boy in the front row, wearing a sweater that looked about three sizes too big for him, was circled in red.

"There isn't anything that says who they were," David remarked, looking at the photo over her shoulder.

"But I'd be willing to bet that's Michael Smith."

"Who?"

"The boy Beau Richmond said he killed with Walter Hamilton's help."

"Do you really think he killed that boy, Sheriff?"

Sharyn shrugged. "He seemed to believe it. We're going to have to talk to Judge Hamilton."

David whistled through his teeth. "Nobody's gonna like that!"

"I know," she agreed, not seeing any way around it. "Maybe now would be a good time to appoint an assistant sheriff and go on vacation."

"Not me," he replied firmly. "If we're wrong, it could mean the end for someone's career."

"Even Michaelson has to admit the evidence is too compelling to exclude the judge from the investigation."

"He might admit that," David assured her. "But he won't be the one to lead the way to questioning the judge."

"You're right."

Julia Richmond graced them with her presence

again. In her casual, chic dark suit she looked a little less ethereal. She took Sharyn's hand when she heard they were leaving. "I hope you can find out who did this, Sheriff. Beau didn't deserve to die."

"We'll do our best," Sharyn assured her, her hand swallowing Julia's fingers in her grip.

Julia turned to David. "You've been so wonderful. Maybe you could help me keep up with what's going on in the investigation?"

David glanced at Sharyn, who nodded wryly. "I'll do that, Mrs. Richmond."

"Julia," the woman corrected him. "Beau always told me not to trust a man with a mustache but I think yours is rather interesting. Thank you for your help."

"David," he supplied, fingering his mustache. "Thank you for your cooperation."

David played with his mustache, glancing at it occasionally in the mirror as they drove back to town. Sharyn sighed and wished Ernie would come to his senses. That there could be a link between Ernie, Walter Hamilton, and Beau Richmond nagged at her. It wasn't anything to do with the boy's murder anyway, she decided, turning into the impound lot; otherwise, Beau would've mentioned him in the confession.

Unless he didn't have time before Ernie got to him.

Sharyn refused to allow that thought to enter her

mind. Ernie had worked with her father for twenty years. He'd been like a member of her family. He'd helped her get started when no one else thought she was fit to be sheriff. Ernie Watkins wasn't a murderer.

The snow was mostly gone by mid-afternoon. The roads were clear but wet as the temperatures soared into the seventies. There was water dripping off of everything as the heavy, wet snow melted off roofs, gutters, lampposts, and porches. The sky was so blue, it hurt people's eyes to look at it against the sun-brightened snow. The frozen precipitation had brought down the rest of the red and gold leaves from the trees. They added to the slush and debris already in the street.

"Go home for a few hours," Sharyn told David. "Get some sleep and we'll try to rotate shifts until everyone is caught up."

"Okay. I'll be back by five."

"David," she cautioned as he started out of the Jeep, "I don't have to tell you that what we learned today was confidential, do I?"

"No, ma'am," he replied diligently. "It won't go past my lips."

Sharyn didn't go inside the office. She drove home for a shower, a change of clothes, and a few hours' rest herself. Trudy brought her up to scratch over the phone on what had been going on during the day. Michaelson had made a pest of himself, calling every few hours for updates, but otherwise, Trudy hadn't seen him at the office.

Sharyn saw that her mother's car was gone and that Caison Talbot wasn't anywhere to be seen. She was thankful not to have to see him and Michaelson on the same day. She was just too exhausted to care about much of anything else. She set her alarm clock, climbed into bed, and fell asleep when her head hit the pillow.

THREE HOURS LATER, she was up again. She took a shower and put a frozen dinner in the microwave oven. The sun was already setting and it wasn't even 6:00 p.m. Most of the snow was gone but the roads would freeze that night. She knew her deputies had done what they needed to keep the watch going until things cleared up.

Wrapped in her bathrobe, her hair curly and wet around her face, she sat down to eat her dinner and read the paper. The headlines, of course, were screaming Beau Richmond's death and the fact that the DA's office had taken over the primary investigation. Sharyn sipped at her warm mint tea.

There was a knock at the door and she tightened her bathrobe, thinking how many times Ernie had come for her. She opened the door. It was Nick, standing on the step with her gun in his hand.

"I—uh—brought this for you," he explained badly.

"Thanks," she answered. "You could've left it for me at the office."

"I know."

The silence hung between them. The water dripped from the roof, trying to fill in the conversation gap. He held out the gun and she took it in her hand.

"That's a pretty heavy weapon," he observed.

"It was my grandfather's during the war."

"They make guns lighter and smaller now."

She shrugged. "I can't imagine carrying anything else."

He nodded and looked at his shoes. "I left the nightstick on your desk. I thought you'd like to have the gun. I know it means something to you."

"Thanks," she said again, holding the neck of her robe together with her free hand.

"Would you like to go and get something to eat?" he asked quietly, glancing up into her scrubbed pink face.

"No, thanks. I'm just finishing up. I'm going in for another shift until things get back to normal."

He nodded again. "Yeah."

"You've been going at it for a while," she observed. "You should get some sleep."

"I've picked up a few hours here and there. I have that sofa in my office. It's comfortable."

Sharyn nodded and shifted position in the doorway.

"Sharyn, I want you—" He paused.

"Pardon?"

He shook his head. "I want you...to know that it wasn't me. I didn't tell Michaelson what was going on. I think it might be Jeremy."

"Why?" she asked bluntly.

"Maybe he's paying him. Maybe he promised him my job. I don't know."

It made sense, she supposed. Jeremy was Nick's assistant and he was there at the office last night. He'd only been working with them for a few months. He always seemed to fade into the background. Except when they were working—then he liked to take center stage.

"Okay."

"Okay?" he questioned. "Is that it?"

"What do you want me to say?"

Nick shrugged and started back down the stairs. "I don't know, Sharyn. I'm gonna go home and get some sleep. I'll see you later."

She watched him get in his car and drive away.

She closed the door on the chilly night that was coming and pretended that she didn't care that she saw hurt etched in Nick's dark face.

FIVE

JUDGE WALTER HAMILTON was a stalwart figure of a man. He was at his best in his black robe, sitting behind the big desk in the courthouse, dispensing justice. His favorite historical figure was George Washington. Many people thought he did what he could to look like the father of his country. Even to wearing his thick head of graying hair tied in a small ponytail at the nape of his neck. One thing was certain: Judge Hamilton had never had any outbursts of violence or rhetoric in his courtroom. People were in awe of him.

For the first time in weeks, Ernie offered to accompany Sharyn on business. He said he didn't want her to have to interview the judge alone. He was there early that morning, in a freshly pressed uniform, with a shine on his black shoes. The sprig of hair he had claim to was firmly pushed into place on his head.

"'Morning, Sheriff," he greeted her.

"Ernie," she acknowledged. "You look good this morning."

"Thank you." He looked her over. "You're looking good, too, Sheriff. Are you ready?"

It was as if the past few months hadn't taken place. Sharyn longed to ask him if he had a connection to Walter Hamilton and Beau Richmond but she wasn't sure she wanted to know the answer. If it was incriminating to him, she knew she didn't want to hear. She wanted to believe in coincidence for the first time in her life.

"How's Annie doing?" she asked when they were walking in the mellow sunshine toward the courthouse.

"She's coping," Ernie explained. "It's been hard with her daughter. She doesn't understand why her parents aren't together anymore."

"But it's good with the two of you?" Sharyn continued.

"Yeah." He squinted into the warm sunshine. There was only the barest of traces that snow had fallen. The weather was back to being fall again. "I never thought it could be this way for me."

Sharyn barely knew anything about Ernie's life. She knew that he had never married and had lived with his mother until she'd died the year before. Ernie didn't talk about his personal life much. There might have been things that he shared with her father that he didn't consider appropriate to share with her. He had his rules of decorum, as far as their relationship was concerned.

"I'm happy for you, Ernie," she told him with a smile.

"You should try it," Ernie replied, grinning like a man half his age with his new mustache.

"Don't start, Ernie! I get enough of that from my mother!"

"Speaking of which," Ernie began, "it looks like your mother and Caison are getting pretty close."

"I know." She groaned. "He spends too much time at my house. I don't know what she sees in him."

Ernie laughed. "You should be happy for her. Faye wasn't meant to live alone."

"She doesn't," Sharyn pointed out briefly.

"But someday, you'll probably decide you want a family and a place of your own. This way, she'll have Caison."

"What a thought!"

"You know what I mean!" He laughed, then sobered, looking for all the world like a man with a guilty conscience. "There's something I have to talk to you about, Sheriff. I should have done it already but I couldn't find the words."

"Ernie—"

"You have to let me tell you before it gets out on its own."

Sharyn sighed. "Okay. Go ahead."

Unfortunately, Lennie joined them at that moment. "Thought you could use the backup."

"And you just at the start of your legal career?" Sharyn teased him, relieved yet uncomfortable that Ernie's confession was interrupted.

Lennie nodded. He wore his deputy uniform better than anyone else on the job. He looked like a movie-star version of a deputy sheriff. This morning, with his uniform freshly pressed and cleaned, he looked even more unreal than usual. "I trust you, Sheriff. And your record shows you have some mighty good hunches."

"She's just lucky," Ernie told him plainly.

"Well, I believe her luck will last through this case. If I'm there with her and she's right, Judge Hamilton, and everybody else in Diamond Springs, is gonna remember it."

Ernie laughed. "I don't think I've ever met a man with more honest ambition than you, Lennie!"

"Thanks, Ernie," Lennie said, shaking his hand.

"You haven't talked to David," Sharyn assured him wryly.

Their appointment with the judge was at 9:45. Sharyn knew that meant 9:45 and not 9:47. She'd made that mistake in her first month with Judge Hamilton. He'd thrown her case right out of court. So she walked into his office with her two escorts five minutes early that morning.

"Sheriff Howard to see Judge Hamilton," she told his clerk.

The woman nodded. "I'll tell him, Sheriff."

Sharyn held her hat in nervous fingers. A strong seventh sense was telling her that she wasn't going to like what was said that morning. It was all part of the investigation but she didn't like the circles it was taking.

"The judge will see you now," his clerk told them at exactly 9:45.

The judge's chambers were filled with legal books and heavy, dark furniture. The ever-present pictures of Washington adorned the walls. The judge's desk was of mammoth proportions, dominating the large room.

Judge Hamilton sat behind that desk as though he were sitting behind the bench of the Supreme Court. His dark suit and crisp white shirt were impeccable. His eyes had the quality of steel as they followed them into the room. His graying head was held high and his strong chin was firmly in place. He was not a man to be ignored.

"Sheriff Howard."

"Judge Hamilton."

"Deputy Watkins."

"Judge Hamilton."

The judge looked at Lennie with a polished glare. "I don't believe I know you."

"Lennie Albert." The deputy rushed forward to offer his hand.

The judge considered that outstretched append-age as though it were something distasteful.

"Uh—Leonard, sir." Lennie withdrew his hand and stepped back beside Sharyn and Ernie. "Leonard Albert, sir."

The judge inclined his head. "Deputy Albert." He dismissed the deputy with his eyes, and sat back in his chair. "What can I do for you, Sheriff?"

Sharyn took a seat in one of the big, dark chairs. Ernie and Lennie stood behind her.

"I know you've heard about Beau Richmond's death, sir."

"Yes. A terrible tragedy. It was a suicide, I believe?"

"That's why we're here, sir. The medical examiner has ruled Mr. Richmond's death a murder."

The judge's face paled visibly. He brought his hands down to the arms of his chair and stared at them. "How can that be true? He was being held in the sheriff's office, wasn't he?"

"Actually, sir," Sharyn corrected him, "he wasn't being held. He had walked in and wanted to confess to a murder."

Walter Hamilton got up from his chair and stood at the window with his hands drawn tightly behind his back. "He was a fool."

Despite his granite appearance, Sharyn could see his hands were trembling. "Sir?"

He raised his voice. "Beau Richmond was a fool, Sheriff," he spat at her.

"We thought he was distraught, sir. He was agitated and worried about being able to confess to a crime that night. He told us that he had murdered someone. We thought the suicide, as awful as it was, was his way of dealing with the problem. Until we found that he'd been murdered."

"How?"

"Excuse me, sir?"

"How was he murdered, Sheriff?"

Sharyn watched him closely. "He was hit very hard in the back of the head, then someone hanged him from the ceiling." She noticed, practically, that Judge Hamilton was a very large man. "Cause of death, though, involved the head wound. He was in bad shape before he was hanged."

Judge Hamilton brought his fist down hard on the heavy desk. Ernie, Sharyn, and Lennie jumped slightly. "And why are you telling me this, Sheriff?"

"Well, sir, we found a note, written in his own hand, that confesses to a crime and names you as being an accomplice."

"What?"

"I have a photocopy." Sharyn obliged him by showing him the duplicate. "The real thing, as I'm sure you appreciate, is being held as evidence."

Judge Hamilton glanced at the piece of paper then

rolled it into a ball and tossed it into the trash. "Are you here to arrest me, Sheriff?"

"No, sir. I'm here for some answers."

He sat back down in his chair and faced his accusers. "I have nothing to hide."

Sharyn sat forward. "You were friends with Mr. Richmond?"

"I was. We were friends for more years than you've been alive, young woman!"

She nodded. "You were in Jefferson Training School together, weren't you?"

"We were. Though I should tell you that there were never formal charges put against any of us. It was part of the agreement about going to the school instead of jail. I'll save you the time of looking it up."

"I don't want to make this hard for you, sir. And I don't want to sound like I'm looking for a scandal, so I'm not going to ask why you were there. You and Mr. Richmond were very young."

"It doesn't matter," he said in a weary voice. "Things have a way of catching up with us, Sheriff. I thought this part of my life was dead and buried. I never thought to speak of it again." He smiled. A rare event for the man. Then his lips resumed their natural scowling attitude. "I even thought my years of community service would make up for it. I have given my life to this town!"

Sharyn noticed the significant look Walter Hamilton gave Ernie. Something *meaningful* passed between them. Ernie was involved, somehow, even though Beau hadn't implicated him the way he had the judge. Even though the judge was choosing not to include Ernie either. She didn't understand it but she knew it in her heart. It made her want to break down and cry.

"I was there because I was stupid and wild, Sheriff." He cracked his tight mouth into a semblance of a smile again. "I know it's probably hard for you to believe that about me. But it's true. My parents were farmers, and I thought they didn't know anything. I wanted to go places and do things. I was arrested for stealing a car that Beau and I were going to take to Norfolk. We were going to join the Navy and see the world."

He was right, she admitted to herself. She couldn't imagine him stealing a car and taking Beau Richmond with him to look for excitement.

"They caught up with us just outside of Charlotte. It was a choice of jail or the boys' school. I was only sixteen, like Beau. He'd stolen a pack of cigarettes at the grocer's. We both decided to stay together and go to boys' school."

"Mr. Richmond told us that while the two of you were there, you picked on a younger boy named Michael Smith."

The judge nodded. "He was the building idiot.

Couldn't take care of himself; not smart enough to tie his own shoes, if you know what I mean. He was about ten; they mixed us all together. A building housed about twenty boys then. We picked on him. Stupid pranks, kid stuff, pushing his face in his lunch, putting ants in his bed. All he had to do was help us out and we would've protected him but he just didn't get it."

"Then the games got more violent?"

Walter Hamilton rose again and strode to the window that overlooked the southern face of the old courthouse. He had looked out on that view every day for the past twenty years.

"We smacked him around some. Sometimes, we would put out a foot and trip him as he went down the stairs. I can't tell you that any of it made sense, Sheriff. I can tell you that boys in school today are doing the same stupid things."

Sharyn considered his words. "Mr. Richmond told us that the two of you took Michael Smith out one night and hit him in the head. He said that the boy was dead and that you buried him just below the old bridge."

The judge rounded on her. "And I'm telling you, Sheriff, that Beau was sick. I knew what he was saying about the boy. He called me and told me that Michael was dead that night. He also told me that the boy's ghost was haunting him! Beau was having emotional problems, Sheriff. A breakdown. I don't know what you'd call it. Maybe that young wife of his was driving him crazy. All I do know is that we took Michael Smith down to where they were working on the bridge that night. We smacked him around and fed him some corn liquor we got from an old still the boys kept on the property. We were all drunk. He rolled down the hill and we threw some leaves on him. Then we walked back to the building without him."

"Did you ever see him again?"

"No, but that wasn't unusual. Boys ran away every day. It was a grueling life there. We got up every morning at four and worked all day long. We made everything ourselves, by hand. In a few months, we were all strong as bulls and twice as mean. The big boys picked on the little boys. If you wanted to survive, you learned to fight. But as God is my witness, I know Michael wasn't dead."

Sharyn scrutinized his words carefully. "You seem very sure about that for someone who never saw him alive again."

He looked away from her. "I know that Michael Smith didn't die that night."

"How?"

He refused to budge. "I just *know!*"

"You didn't talk about it at the school after it happened? Brag about it to the other boys?"

"Sure, but we said we scared him into running away. We never said we killed him. I don't know why Beau started thinking that he was dead."

"When was it that Mr. Richmond first came to you with the idea that Michael was dead and that the two of you had killed him?"

"The first time was about two months ago. We talked about it on and off after that. I tried to convince him to get help. He wouldn't listen. He just wanted to ruin his life, and apparently mine, with this nonsense."

Sharyn nodded and stood up to leave.

"I'm sure I don't need to remind you to keep this under your hat, Sheriff," the judge said absolutely. "If word of this gets out, my reputation would be ruined and there's no evidence that any crime was committed. If that happens, I'd be forced to sue the sheriff's office for slander."

Sharyn nodded. "Sir, I think you should know that just before the snow really hit, we found the skeletal remains of a young boy draped across the cross at the front of the boys' chapel at Jefferson Training School. The medical examiner believes that he was probably about ten, that he was buried for a while. The back of his skull was crushed. The medical examiner's office sent it away for more detailed study and they're checking the records at the boys' school."

"Are you threatening me, Sheriff?" Judge Hamilton demanded, drawing himself up to his full height. His fierce blue eyes collided with her own forthright gaze.

"No, sir," she promised. "I'm telling you where we are with this case. If you've told me the truth, there shouldn't be any problem."

"No problem? I think there could be a problem, Sheriff! I think someone is trying to kill me."

"What makes you think that, sir?"

He shrugged and adjusted his suit. "The brakes failed on my car. I'd just had them repaired and they failed. I was coming down the big hill from my house and they gave out. I would have gone right into the lake if it hadn't been for an embankment that I rolled up on. The loose dirt slowed the car and finally stopped it. But my mechanic told me that it looked like the brake fluid had been let out of the brakes."

"Or your mechanic forgot to put some in it?" she suggested. "You did just have them worked on, sir."

He pounded the desk with his fist again and glared at her. "Don't make light of this, Sheriff! Someone could be out to kill me as well. It might have nothing to do with this Michael Smith thing!"

"Who would that be, sir?" she wondered.

"Possibly someone loosely connected to Beau. Someone I've sent to jail. I get death threats all the time. I'm sure I have enemies!"

"I'll leave my deputy here to take your statement and get the details, sir. Lennie, could you take down what happened to the judge?"

"I could do that, Sheriff," Ernie volunteered. He flipped out his notepad.

Sharyn looked at Ernie. "All right," she agreed. "I'll let you know what happens, sir."

"Thank you, Sheriff. I know you'll put the proper emphasis on investigating this case!"

"Of course, sir. One last question? Where were you night before last during the storm?"

"Where I should have been, Sheriff. At home, so I wasn't out causing more problems on the road."

"Were you alone, sir?"

"No, my wife was with me."

"Thank you, sir." She nodded.

Sharyn looked back once at Ernie standing beside the judge's desk. Then she closed the door behind her as she and Lennie left the room. A terrible feeling of impending doom was sitting hard on her chest. She couldn't shake it.

"What do you think?" Lennie asked her when they were back out in the sunshine again.

"I don't know," she answered warily. "If Beau was threatening to go public without the judge's consent, Judge Hamilton said it himself, it would ruin his career, even if nothing was proven."

"So you're saying the judge could have sneaked in there that night and brained Beau to keep him from telling people about his fantasy?"

"It's possible," Sharyn told him. "And that's saying that the child's death *is* a fantasy. What did you think?"

"I think the judge is the kind of man who'd hire someone to do a job like that," Lennie expressed. "He doesn't strike me as the kind to sneak in while the lights are low and hit a man in the back of the head and hang him."

"I agree. But he still had motive and opportunity. He's been in the office enough that he knows that we keep the key to the conference room on the wall."

"He has an alibi," Lennie reminded her.

"As much as a wife can give him," she replied quietly.

They walked up the steps and into the sheriff's department. Ed was bringing in a man for running his truck into his neighbor's front room because the neighbor kept playing his trumpet at night. Joe was writing the report. Things were mostly back to normal with the weather warmer and the snow gone from the streets.

"Sheriff," Trudy said when she saw her, "ADA Michaelson called to remind you that you haven't called him. Twice. Your mother called to tell you that your sister is home early. And Nick is in your office."

"Thanks, Trudy. Will you order lunch in for me, please?"

"Yes, ma'am. What happened to Ernie?"

"He's taking the judge's statement. He should be back soon."

Sharyn opened the door to her office and found Nick sitting at her desk as usual, with his feet up on the desk. Lennie walked in behind her and closed the door.

"Nick."

"Sharyn."

She stared meaningfully at his feet and he smiled.

"I need to talk to you."

"Okay."

He glanced at Lennie's dark, handsome face behind her. "Alone."

Sharyn balked at first. After all, if anyone was feeding Michaelson information, it seemed to be Nick. "Lennie's part of the investigation."

"Sharyn—"

"I'll go over for lunch," Lennie suggested with a brilliant smile at Nick. "I'm sure Sharyn can tell me whatever it is later."

"And I'm sure you can—" Nick started to his feet.

"Never mind," Sharyn interrupted them. "Len-

nie, get the address from Trudy and when you finish lunch, take a ride out to Judge Hamilton's house
and talk to his wife."

"Okay," Lennie complied readily. "Anything else
I can do for you, Sharyn?"

"Not right now," she answered. "Thanks."

Lennie nodded at Nick. "See you later."

"You bet."

The door closed behind Lennie. Nick stood up and
walked around the big desk. "What is it with him?"

"What do you mean?" she asked coolly.

"He's around you like a schoolboy with a crush
on the teacher."

Sharyn laughed and hung up her hat and gun. "I
don't think so. He works for me."

"You don't see it because you're prejudiced."

"You mean because he does a good job?"

"I mean because he's an ex–football player with
a great body and a pretty face."

She laughed again. "Well! Is he all over me or am
I all over him?"

"Never mind."

"Good." She sat down at her desk. "What do you
want, Nick?"

He took a seat in front of the desk, facing her, and
opened his briefcase. "Report back from Raleigh
about the remains found at the chapel. The bones

do belong to a boy around ten years old, dead about twenty years."

"About?" Sharyn asked with a frown.

"Yeah." He looked up at her. "Is that a problem for you?"

"Well, if Beau and Judge Hamilton killed a boy at the school forty years ago, this couldn't be his skeleton."

Nick shrugged. "Ten years one way or another is possible. The skeleton was in serious decay, obviously left in the ground for a long time. It was also moved before. There was evidence of different soil on it."

"So, you're saying this could be Michael Smith's body?"

"I'm saying it's possible. The only way to tell will be the dental records. The school kept fingerprints and dental records for each boy. Jeremy is checking through them now. But it's gonna take a while. There were a lot of boys in that school, and the records are old and poorly kept."

"Okay. I don't think Judge Hamilton is going anywhere, so I can wait for that," she said. "Anything else?"

He laid out another report for her. "The chapel. Beau's fingerprints were everywhere, on everything. Outside of a few prints we matched to the maintenance workers and Mrs. Fine, they were the only fresh prints there. The remains were covered with them. Apparently, Beau put them there to get attention."

"He wanted to go public with what happened," she surmised. "I guess he couldn't think of a better way."

"Why didn't he just bring them in with him when he confessed?" Nick wondered. "Why the drama of draping them on the cross in the chapel?"

Sharyn shook her head. "I don't know. Maybe coming to the station and confessing was an afterthought. I think we've established that he wasn't in his normal frame of mind."

"How's that?"

She looked at him without responding.

Nick glared back. "You can't honestly think I'm feeding Michaelson information behind your back? What about Jeremy? What about your precious Lennie?"

"I don't know, Dr. Thomopolis, but I think we've established that Michaelson has a *very* high regard for you."

"Sharyn." He paused, then began gathering his things together. "No. I'm not even going there. If you're so stubborn and so blind that you can't see how I feel about—"

"What?"

"Never mind!" He jammed the briefcase lid down

without getting everything inside. "I don't know why I didn't resign when you took office! I don't know why I'm hanging around here."

"Nick—"

"I'll be at the college all afternoon, if you need me. Or if you prefer, Jeremy is at the office. I'm sure he can help you more than I can."

"Nick—"

Ed knocked quickly then pushed open the office door. "Sheriff, Judge Hamilton was almost killed by a piece of stonework that fell off the courthouse as he walked by! He's hollering like a stuck pig for you. Better come quick!"

Sharyn followed her deputy into the street. Nick ran behind them. A crowd had gathered around the sidewalk where the statuary fell. Traffic on Main Street had slowed to a crawl.

"Ernie, get that crowd out of the way," she told him as he ran out of the courthouse.

"Yes, ma'am."

"Ed, keep that traffic moving. Do we need an ambulance? Was anyone hurt?"

"I don't think so," he returned.

"Why weren't you with the judge?" she asked Ernie as he began to clear the crowd.

"I finished talking with him. He said he was going out for lunch. I went to the restroom. I heard the commotion and ran out here."

"Sheriff!" Judge Hamilton called from the center of the crowd. "Sheriff Howard!"

"Yes, sir," Sharyn yelled back, wading through the large group of people. She looked back at Nick. "Will you come with me in case he's been hurt?"

He nodded and moved in close behind her.

Lennie came running out of the diner. "Sheriff?"

"Help Ernie with this crowd," she advised him. "Ed can handle the street."

When Sharyn and Nick finally reached the judge, he was sitting down on the wooden bus-stop bench. The fallen piece of statuary was at his feet. It was easily ten feet high and four feet across. Sharyn had no idea what it weighed, but any part of it would have killed the judge if it had hit him.

"What did I tell you, Sheriff?" the judge wheezed. "I told you someone is trying to kill me!"

"Are you injured, sir?" she asked him. "Did any of it hit you?"

"No. But it only missed me by a fraction of an inch! Someone is trying to kill me!"

"Sit back, sir, and let me take a look at you," Nick said, checking his pulse.

"I'm not hurt," the judge insisted. "Just scared and winded! I'm having a little trouble catching my breath."

The sound of the ambulance arrived over the edge

of the crowd that Ernie and Lennie still hadn't been able to disperse.

"He's probably fine," Nick pronounced. "His pulse is fast. But he's had a scare."

"It won't hurt to take him in," Sharyn decided.

"What? There's no reason for me to go to the hospital," Judge Hamilton told them squarely. "I don't need to go anywhere. I just need someone to protect me."

The judge ranted but he went with the paramedics, who had him lie back on a stretcher and loaded him into the ambulance.

"There's probably a few people here who saw what happened," Sharyn told Ernie, Lennie, and Ed. "Let's get some statements, huh?"

Jeremy ran toward them down the sidewalk. He was clearly breathing hard as he tried to reach them. "Is everyone all right?" he asked.

"I think so," Sharyn told him. She looked up toward the top of the courthouse. "I think we need to find out how that statue fell down."

"I can handle that for you, Sheriff," Jeremy volunteered. "I can take a team up there and we can check it out."

Sharyn glanced at Nick, who shrugged and looked away. "That's fine, Jeremy. I'd appreciate it."

"Thanks, Sheriff," he said with a big smile. "I appreciate your confidence in me. I know I made a mistake with Mr. Richmond, but I was right about the child in the chapel. Sometimes, I just get a little eager."

"I know. Thanks, Jeremy."

He smiled and ran off again, heading back to the hospital to round up a team.

"I don't know for sure if he can handle it," Nick said to Sharyn.

"If he's going to be your assistant, I guess he'd better learn," she answered. "I fought too hard with the board to get him here for you to give up on him."

"We could fire him and try again?" Nick suggested.

"Have you seen the statistics on employment lawsuits for counties?"

"Okay." He shrugged. "I'll just look over everything he does."

"Thanks. He's bound to improve."

"At least he can't kill anybody," Nick quipped. "They're already dead."

Ed laughed out loud. "That's a good one, Nick!"

Sharyn shook her head. "I'm going to check on the judge."

"I brought your lunch, Sheriff," Lennie told her. "I was right there anyway."

Nick gave her an I-told-you-so glance then went to find his car. "I'm starting my class on some dental records from Jefferson this afternoon. I'll let you know if anything turns up."

"Nick—" she started.

He shook his head and kept walking. "Forget it. I'll talk to you later."

"Don't think we're gonna get any prints off this, Sheriff," Ernie told her, squinting at the smashed statue on the ground.

"Probably not," she agreed. "Did anyone see what happened?"

Ernie looked at Ed. "He lucked out. Both of those women were behind the judge when the statue fell. But I doubt if either of them were looking at the top of the courthouse."

"Maybe they saw something else," she said. "It's all we have right now anyway."

"Courthouse is old," Ernie added. "I don't think a statue falling down makes it attempted murder, even if the judge was under it."

"Two close calls, though, Ernie," she reminded him. "Could you go out and have a talk with the judge's mechanic?"

"Sure thing, Sheriff. I'm meeting Annie for lunch, then I'll go out that way."

Joe waved as he brought in a drunk driver he'd caught on the Interstate. Sharyn took her lunch from Lennie.

"I'm on my way to the judge's house," he said. "Want me to poke around a little, too?"

"Not right now," she replied. "Just find out about

the night of the blizzard. I want to know what they were doing and how tight her alibi is for him."

"You still think the judge might have killed Beau Richmond, even after the statuary fell on him?"

"It wouldn't be the first time," she answered. "I'll talk to you later."

SIX

THE DOCTOR ON CALL at the emergency room reported that the judge was shaken but unharmed. Lennie was on his way to interview the judge's wife, but she was already at the hospital when Sharyn arrived there.

Ellen Hamilton was standing at her husband's bedside when the nurse brought Sharyn to see him. The judge was resting comfortably but ready to leave.

"Sheriff Howard," his wife greeted her with a gracious smile. "I was at the fund-raising event the night of the blizzard. I spoke with you briefly."

"I remember," Sharyn said, recognizing her. "It's been an eventful few days."

"I'll say! I declare, you've been busy!"

"Get on with it," Judge Hamilton said angrily. "This isn't a social! I know you want to ask her if I was home with her that night, Sheriff. Quit beating around the bush."

"What's this about, Sheriff?" Mrs. Hamilton wondered curiously.

"It's about a murder that was committed at the sheriff's office the night of the blizzard, Mrs. Hamilton."

The older woman looked at her husband. "You don't suspect Walter, do you?"

"She does, Ellen," the judge admitted. His craggy brow furrowed. "And possibly not without reason."

"I can't believe it," Ellen Hamilton stated defiantly. "After all the years my husband has given to this community! How could he be suspected of murder?"

"It was Beau Richmond, Ellen," her husband started to explain.

"I realize Beau was killed, Walt. I read the paper. I just don't see why the sheriff would suspect you!"

Judge Hamilton sighed. "She doesn't know the circumstances, Sheriff."

"What circumstances?" Mrs. Hamilton looked back and forth between her husband and Sharyn.

Sharyn smiled. "I'm going to leave that to your husband to explain, Mrs. Hamilton. All I need to ask you is if your husband was with you that night and what you were doing."

"Well," Ellen began, then faltered. "We went to bed early because the weather was so bad. I got in from the fund-raiser about eight or nine. I didn't stay late. Walter was already home. The power went off early out our way. We went to bed about ten and slept through until morning."

"Anyone else in the house?" Sharyn asked hopefully.

"No. Corinne comes in every day but she always leaves by six. Our son is away at school." She looked at Sharyn. "There was no one else. But I was asleep at his side all night, Sheriff. I'm a very light sleeper."

"All right," Sharyn said, putting away her notebook.

"Not much of an alibi, huh, Sheriff?" the judge demanded. "Maybe when *I'm* dead, too, you'll do better out looking for my murderer. Because at this rate, you'll never find who killed Beau!"

"Walter!" his wife cautioned, appalled by his words.

"Thanks," Sharyn said, putting on her hat. "Sorry to trouble you."

"Are you checking out my other story?" the judge wondered. "Are you talking to the mechanic about my brakes?"

"As a matter of fact, sir, we are," she promised. "I'll let you know what we find."

"Let me know when you find the killer," he replied. "Don't bother me with the details."

Sharyn left the hospital, not liking what she'd heard inside. The judge essentially had no alibi. She didn't really think he could be involved in Beau's death but she knew Michaelson was going to be looking for news soon. Fortunately for the judge, it was going to take something more incriminating for Michaelson to want to make a move against him. Judge Hamilton was a powerful man in the county. He was respected and well liked, almost an institution. He was bound to have powerful friends.

In the sunshine again, Sharyn started back toward the office, when two hands came from behind and covered her eyes.

"Guess who?"

"Kristie!" she said and spun around to hug her sister. "I heard you were home."

"But you couldn't take a few minutes to say hello?" her younger sister despaired. "I'm not as important as a hot murder lead? You're as bad as Dad was!"

Sharyn laughed. "Not when it's Judge Hamilton."

Kristie's blue eyes widened dramatically in her tanned young face. "Judge 'George Washington' Hamilton? You're kidding!"

"I wish I were! When did you get back?"

"Last night. Caison and Mom took me out for lunch at Tony's, then I let them drive back and leave me to wander around a little bit. I thought they could use the time alone, you know?"

Sharyn grimaced. "Don't remind me."

"What do you have against Caison?" Kristie wondered, falling into step beside her sister. "He's wealthy, powerful, devoted to Mom, likes to take her out for a good time. Dad would've approved, I think. Why don't you?"

"I don't disapprove," Sharyn told her. "I just don't see Caison Talbot in that golden light you just painted over his head."

Kristie laughed. "Don't you want Mom to be happy, Sharyn? She seems really happy with him."

"Mom is happy when anybody pays attention to her," Sharyn disputed, noticing that Kristie took about the same size stride as she. They were almost the same height but where Sharyn had her father's stocky build, Kristie had her mother's delicate body.

"So? What's wrong with that? Nobody wants to be alone."

"I know, Kristie," Sharyn confided. "I've just run up against Caison too many times. He's sneaky and devious. He'll do anything to get his own way."

"Sounds exciting to me," Kristie said with a smile. "Seriously, Sharyn, Mom told me you were busy. I stopped to see you because Mom is going to ask you to go out to dinner tonight with me and Caison. She said she knew you wouldn't go because you always say no. So how about saying yes, for me? How about declaring a truce and wanting to see Mom happy?"

Sharyn looked at her sister's bright eyes and perfect smile. "All right. What time?"

Kristie hugged her. "Seven. At Fuigi's, so get home early and change, okay? Mom will probably call and ask you later. Let's just be a family tonight, huh? We haven't been much of one since Dad died, Sharyn."

"I'll be there, Kristie, but I can't promise to ever think of Caison as family."

"Well, at least smile and keep your mouth shut, then," Kristie said with a laugh. "I'm going to have a soda with Keith."

"The boy you left behind?"

"Yeah," Kristie admitted, wiggling her eyebrows suggestively. "He's looking *good!*"

Sharyn laughed and watched Kristie sashay down the sidewalk. She had managed to avoid going out with the senator and her mother for two months. The first night Kristie comes back, and they were all going out as a family.

"YOUR MOTHER CALLED," Trudy informed her as she walked into the sheriff's department. "And Michaelson is waiting for you in your office."

"Thanks," Sharyn responded. "Remind me to get a lock for that door!"

Michaelson was waiting for her, looking through the case files at her desk. Sharyn hung up her hat and gun and glanced at the picture of her father on the wall. She wondered if he would really approve of his old friend Caison Talbot marrying his wife. She knew her father was a pragmatic man. He probably knew that Faye couldn't be alone for long.

"I've been studying the report of the forensics findings on the conference room after the murder," Michaelson told her without preamble.

"I haven't seen those yet."

He didn't look up. "There were no fingerprints besides those of the people who work here. The belt around Beau Richmond's neck was clean. They couldn't find anything useful on his body."

"Thanks for the update." She sank into a chair at the front of her desk. "I suppose you heard about the judge?"

"The attack on his life? Yeah. Not much of an attack."

"What did you have in mind?" she wondered. "A sniper in the courthouse?"

Michaelson looked up at her. "I don't think either of us wants to bring in the judge for this murder. If we're wrong, it could hurt both of us."

"But I think you have to admit that the sheriff's department is clean in all of this," Sharyn persuaded. "There's isn't anything to implicate anyone in my department."

"Not yet," Michaelson admitted. "But there's always tomorrow."

"David was an idiot," she told him. "He was wrong

and he'll be written up for it. That doesn't make any of us murderers."

"An idiot and a liar," he reminded her bluntly. "First his statement said that he was gone for five minutes, then half an hour to an hour. Dr. Thomopolis says that it took Richmond an hour to die. How does that fit into your deputy's statements?"

"It doesn't. And I'm not making excuses for him. He was wrong to leave the room without letting me know or asking someone else to step inside to take his place. And I was wrong for not thinking about having someone relieve him. The truth is that it was total chaos here that night. We didn't see anyone slip in or out. Is that what you want to hear?"

"It's a start but it still doesn't solve our problem. I've looked through everything you have so far, Sheriff. None of the volunteers or the deputies knew Beau Richmond or had any contact with him. Except for you, of course. You had dinner with him at the fundraiser."

"Not exactly with him, but he was there," she admitted, wondering where he was going.

"What about your guest, Leonard Albert, the ex-football hero? Have you checked into his background? He might want the young Mrs. Richmond to be the future Mrs. Albert."

Sharyn sat back in her chair. "At that rate, we

could probably find something to link anyone to Beau's murder."

Michaelson smiled. "Not anyone, Sheriff. Just the right one."

"They've found evidence that the remains we found at the old chapel did belong to a young boy."

"That wasn't much of a surprise," Michaelson scoffed. "And I don't think it's related to the crime itself."

"What?"

"All that blathering from Beau Richmond about killing a child forty years ago is just so much garbage. Look deeper, Sheriff. I'm sure there was another link to Beau and one of these people."

"But not the judge? Even though he admitted to at least hurting the young boy forty years ago?"

Michaelson stood abruptly. "I don't want try another case like that plane-in-the-lake case, Sheriff. Old murders don't make big headlines. There's another link that you're missing. I'd advise you to find it. Make us both look good."

He left her and Sharyn stayed in the chair facing her desk. She thought a few more minutes about Michaelson's link. She prayed that it wasn't Ernie. Then she picked up the phone and called her mother.

"I'd like you to go out with us tonight, Sharyn,"

her mother invited. "Caison and I are taking Kristie out for dinner. She's only home a few days."

"All right."

"I know you don't like him but I think you could manage to put a good face on it for your sister's sake, if not for mine," Faye Howard continued.

"Okay."

"Sharyn?"

"I said all right, Mom. I'll go," Sharyn repeated. "When?"

"Seven at Fuigi's. You know Kristie loves that place. Give yourself enough time to change. And dress decently, Sharyn."

"All right."

Faye Howard paused. "Is something wrong, Sharyn?"

"No, Mom."

Faye Howard was unsure but she decided to let it go. She'd never understood her oldest daughter. "All right, then. Tonight at seven at Fuigi's."

Sharyn put down the phone and tried to envision the conversation between her mother and Caison about her accepting their dinner invitation. Somehow, it was hard for her to imagine that Caison wanted her at dinner any more than she wanted to be there.

Lennie knocked at the door then walked into the office. "Safe to come in now?"

"Maybe for a minute or two," she invited. "What's up?"

"Since I found out that the judge's wife was at the hospital and I knew you were going there, too, I thought I might as well check on some other stuff."

"Like?"

Lennie put down two reports on her desk. "I found these at the bank. It's an electronic transfer from Judge Hamilton to Beau Richmond."

Sharyn glanced at the papers. "Twenty-five-thousand dollars?"

He nodded. "I looked at the report again. Two weeks ago, the date of the transfer, is when the judge says Beau came to him again about killing Michael Smith. Right after, he paid him off."

"Or gave him the money for an investment," Sharyn considered.

"Maybe. It's a big coincidence, though."

Sharyn agreed. "We'll have to check into it further. I'm on my way out to the school to take a look around the grounds. Beau must've taken that body from somewhere. We can take a look by the bridge and see what's there. Maybe we can corroborate the story a little better."

"Want me to come?" Lennie asked.

Sharyn glanced at her watch. It was only 2:15. "Sure. Let me see who else is in the office."

Ed went with them. They picked up Jeremy at the hospital since Nick was still in class. If they did find something, Sharyn wanted to be sure it was documented and preserved.

The school grounds were muddy but clear of snow. The old campus included ten large, gray stone dormitories that looked like big three-story houses. There were two barns, workshops, and a cafeteria. The chapel was across the road, accessible only by the stone bridge. The barns were all but destroyed by weather and neglect. The workshops were falling apart. The dormitories were still standing and looked sound, but yellow alert ribbons told a different story. All but one of the buildings were considered unsafe by the county. The other building was used as an office while the county decided what to do with the whole thing.

The parcel of land itself was valuable, even out in the country. Harmony was the closest town to the school. It was a rapidly growing community. The land could be used for new schools or sold. There was a petition to save the old campus, built in 1879, and preserve it as an historic landmark. Sharyn had seen the paperwork for it and signed the petition but she hadn't heard anything else about it.

There was a ghostly, unused feeling to the old

place. It had been empty for almost ten years while the county squabbled over what to do with it. Juvenile crime was different now. Young perpetrators were treated in mental hospitals or sent to detention facilities. Jefferson had been the first of its kind in the country but its ideals had died in the last generation.

"The road was put in after the time the judge and Mr. Richmond were here," Sharyn said as they approached the bridge.

"Actually," Jeremy corrected her, "I read that the road was going to be built and that's why they had the boys build the bridge. They didn't want them walking outside the grounds to get to the chapel."

"Thanks," Sharyn said with a smile. "Anyway, if Beau dug up that skeleton, it was probably from the side of the hill that slopes down to the street. Even with the snow and the mud, we should be able to find some sign of the earth being disturbed."

"My uncle was here for a few months when his parents died," Ed said, slipping down the hillside beside Sharyn. "He said it was a mean place full of mean kids."

Jeremy slipped and fell in the mud but he got up quickly and brushed off his clothes. "I read that most of the boys who survived being here said they would rather have gone to prison."

"Prisons weren't a picnic then either," Lennie said

doubtfully. "It was a tough time to be a criminal. Not like today."

"Criminal-justice system too easy for you, Lennie?" Sharyn asked.

He nodded. "Too many people going in and out too quickly. Nobody's learning anything. The idea that we could reform people should have been over years ago. When has anyone heard of a criminal we've reformed?"

"You would make a good DA," Sharyn advised him. "There's a lot of law enforcement that will side with you on that issue."

"Thanks." He grinned. "Michaelson's an idiot. He thinks political maneuvering will get him reelected. People want to see results. I could beat him with my hands tied together."

The snow had made the hillside muddy and slippery with heaps of wet, dead leaves underfoot. Sharyn was down on her hands and knees before the first half hour. It was easier than trying to stand up. Lennie continued to slide and fall, but Ed and Jeremy were following Sharyn's lead.

"It wouldn't take much room for those small bones to be buried," Jeremy told them. "All we have to do is find a hollowed-out area about three feet long. The bones were in bad condition. Animals had been gnawing on them. It's hard to imagine that even other children would leave a child here."

"Adults don't have the edge on meanness," Ed told him, shifting aside some rocks and leaves. "I know kids that make adult murderers look like babies. Kids can be tough."

"When I think about that poor boy, lying out here, shivering in the night cold as animals tore at his flesh, it makes me shudder." Jeremy stared at the hillside in front of him.

"Are you all right?" Sharyn asked, putting a hand on his shoulder as his gaze didn't waver and the moments passed.

He blinked then smiled at her. "I'm fine. Sometimes it just gets to me, Sheriff. Doesn't it ever bother you?"

Sharyn frowned. "All the time. I have nightmares about it."

"But you do the job."

"I do the job because of the nightmares," she confided. "I want to make a difference and maybe keep another little boy from being put out here."

Jeremy studied her face intently. "That's a noble cause, Sheriff," he commended. "You're a very good person."

"Thanks," she said. "I try to do my job."

"Hey, I think I found something," Lennie called from the opposite side of the hill.

They crossed the street that had been put in as the main street into Harmony almost forty years ago. It had only been used for about five years though, when the U.S. highway system had decided to go through town. Now it was only used by a few people who lived close to the school.

Lennie showed them the burrow-like space he'd found in the hillside. It was about two and a half feet long and cut out of the dirt and clay. Jeremy examined it carefully but pronounced that it couldn't be the place.

"The clay and dirt have been open to the air for too long," he explained to them. "If the body had been closed in here and recently dug out, we would see some mold and pieces of clothing and bone. The body was here for forty years, according to the accounts. The soil would have weathered much differently with the decaying corpse in it."

"Thanks, Jeremy," Sharyn said with a sigh. "We've pretty well been over this area."

"What about the cemetery?" Lennie suggested.

"But Michael Smith was buried out here," Sharyn said.

"But I read that there were some boys who weren't accounted for. I even read that some boys were buried in the cemetery when they died and their parents weren't informed. Maybe they found his body when they put the road through but didn't question who it was. He was a young boy. This was Jefferson Training School. Maybe they just buried him."

"Worth a look, I suppose," Ed assumed. "We couldn't find anything about the boy dying in the records but that doesn't mean it didn't happen."

"Not right now," Sharyn said, glancing at her watch. "It's already five. After the extra hours with the storm, we can't afford to put in extra time on the clock. The commissioners will be down my throat! Ed, take Lennie and Jeremy back to the office and I'll take a look out here."

"How will you get back?" Ed wondered.

She glanced up at the only school building still being used. There were lights on in the windows and plenty of county trucks still rolling in from the road. "I'll hitch a ride back. If you get back now, we can still have a normal shift tomorrow."

"I can stay with you," Lennie offered.

"I need you tomorrow," she told him. "I'll be fine."

"I could send David back for you." Ed tried another tack.

"David." She sighed. "Let's just leave it this way, Ed. I'll find a way back to the office."

Finally, reluctantly, they left her there at the school grounds with twilight beginning to fall. Sharyn tramped through the mud, thinking about David. She was not going to have a choice. Michaelson had made that clear today. She was going to have to reprimand David formally for his actions the night of the storm. Anything else would reflect badly on the department.

She admitted to herself that she was handling David carefully. He'd already left once and she had worked hard on their relationship. He'd been with the department for two years before her father was killed and she'd taken his place as sheriff. David had always seen this as a miscarriage of justice, and their relationship had been difficult.

But she couldn't protect him from his own mistakes. Leaving Beau Richmond had been one of those mistakes. A big one, as it turned out. The commissioners could even demand his resignation. She hoped to forestall that with a reprimand. It only took two to lose the job. David was a good man. He was just careless sometimes.

The little cemetery that belonged to the school was located at the back of the property. Sharyn dropped by the office on her way and asked a driver to wait for her. With the light fading, she wouldn't have long to check out the spot. But she felt it wouldn't take long to locate an open grave.

Headstones had fallen over on the ground and some had splintered into pieces. Last year's weeds were standing skeletons against the cool breeze. Ice crystals had formed on the frozen ground beneath the spreading oak trees where the sun never shined. It was a lonely spot that had obviously been neglected in recent years. One pathetic wreath of artificial flowers clung tenaciously to a headstone near the front, proof that someone had been there recently. The small headstone read:

Matthew Tyler
Age nine
Gone but not forgotten

It was more than Michael Smith had, she reminded herself. She stooped to look at the headstone that was dated 1916 and wondered who was still alive to care for that poor child's grave. As she stood up, something hard hit her in the back of the head and she staggered, falling to one knee in the wet leaves. She thought at first that she had been struck by a low-hanging tree branch. She looked back but there was only darkness....

Slowly, there were lights and voices. Ernie was there and a paramedic she knew from earlier that day when the judge had almost been hit by the statue.

"What's going on?" she wondered.

"I came out to find you after Ed and Lennie got back to the office," he explained. "Did you faint or something?"

"Not with this goose egg on the back of her head," the paramedic told him succinctly. "Somebody hit her with something."

"Nice guess," Ernie said, looking at the knot on Sharyn's head in the flashlight's beam.

"Well, she didn't just walk into something with the back of her head."

"I thought it was a tree branch," she explained, putting a hand to her aching head.

They shined their flashlights upward. The closest tree branch was a good four feet away from where she lay on the ground.

"Let's take her in," the paramedic told his partner. "BP is good but she needs an X-ray, maybe a CT."

"What time is it, Ernie?" Sharyn wondered.

"About six. Why?"

"I can't have anything done right now," she explained. "I have to go to dinner with my mother. I promised."

"She'll understand," Ernie said, siding with the medical personnel. "You've been hurt, Sheriff. You need looking after."

"You don't understand," she protested.

"I know the rules, Sheriff," he answered firmly. "You have to go to the hospital and make sure you're fit for duty."

Sharyn knew that he was right but she knew her mother and sister were going to be furious. They would never believe that she hadn't set it up on purpose to avoid dinner with Caison.

Ernie rode in the ambulance with her after calling into the station.

"What wasn't I supposed to find out there, Ernie?" she wondered aloud.

"What?"

"I was about to look for an open grave in the cemetery that might have been where Beau got the remains he used to get attention. What wasn't I supposed to see?"

"I don't know, Sheriff. Just rest now."

She leaned her head back and looked at the top of the ambulance as it went down the road, sirens blaring and lights flashing.

"And why not kill me, too? It was basically the same method he used to kill Beau. He could have killed me, Ernie. Why did he just stop me?"

"Maybe he likes you," Ernie suggested, worried that she was hurt more than he'd suspected and talking out of her head. "Maybe he didn't need to kill you, just slow you down."

"That could be it," she guessed. "Maybe he picked up whatever he didn't want me to see. Maybe I wasn't supposed to be there yet."

"Just rest, Sheriff, please," Ernie pleaded. "We're almost at the hospital."

"He must have left something in the grave, Ernie. Something he didn't want me to see," she speculated, half rising from the stretcher.

"Sharyn." Ernie spoke in a voice of quiet authority, putting his hands on her arms. "Please. Lie back until they examine you. If you're seriously hurt, you could do more damage. We can go and look for whatever it is tomorrow."

"It's probably already gone," she theorized, not listening to him about her injury. "He probably hit me, then took whatever it was. What could it have been, Ernie?"

Ernie finally managed to take a deep breath when the ambulance stopped and the back doors opened. "I don't know, Sheriff, but we'll look later. For right now, just get better. Okay?"

"Ernie?" Sharyn asked plaintively. "Call my mother, please."

Ernie agreed then watched as they took her into the emergency room. He glanced skyward at the bright stars and thanked heaven that she was still alive.

Sharyn let them poke her and prod her and run her head through various machines for almost forty-five minutes. At 7:20, she signed herself out of the hospital against her doctor's wishes. Dr. Elizabeth Anderson swore that she would file a complaint with the sheriff's department and the county, and that Sharyn would never work in that town again as sheriff. She cited every rule and regulation but nothing fazed her patient. In the end, Sharyn left and took a taxi to her house.

By 7:40, she was standing in the foyer of Fuigi's wearing a long black skirt and powder-blue sweater. She was unsteady on her feet and her head hurt. She knew it was just as well that she had missed dinner because her stomach was doing a dance that was making her nauseated. But she was there. She asked the host for the senator's table. He nodded and took her there.

"Sharyn!" her mother said when she saw her daughter. "Ernie said you were hurt on the job and wouldn't be able to come for dinner."

"Did he mention that it wasn't serious?" she asked with what she hoped was a lighthearted manner. "You know how the regs are, though. Everything has to be checked out." She started to sit down, stumbled a little, but finally managed the feat. She told the waiter she'd just have water with lime, then faced her family with a smile.

"What happened?" Kristie asked, looking at her sister's pale face.

"I was checking out the old cemetery at the Jefferson School and got hit in the head."

"Did someone try to kill you?" Kristie asked enthusiastically.

"I don't think so," Sharyn denied. "I think I walked into a low-hanging branch."

"My daughter." Faye Howard smiled serenely. "All grace and sunshine."

"She does a very good job as sheriff of Diamond Springs," Caison Talbot rose to her defense. "It's a hard time right now with the growth spurt and all. The whole county is shifting, and the sheriff's office is in the middle of it."

"Sharyn is always in the middle of it," Faye observed. "But you look good tonight, dear." She apprised Sharyn. "Even if you are almost an hour late."

"Sharyn was hurt, Mom," Kristie reminded her.

"She said herself it wasn't anything serious or she wouldn't be here," Faye concluded. "It would be nice if once in a while, Sharyn gave us the consideration she gives her job."

"She's like Dad." Kristie shot her sister a smile. "That's why she's so good at it. Nothing is more important than saving Diamond Springs from disaster!"

"Not even her own life," her mother murmured.

Caison patted Faye's hand. "So, how is the investigation going?"

"All right, I guess," Sharyn said, wishing her head would stop hurting. "Better if the DA would get out of my back pocket."

"Jack Winter is bothering you?"

"No, his hired gun is living in my office," she

answered. "Michaelson always does Winter's dirty work. I never see Jack Winter."

He nodded. "Michaelson is a little ambitious and eager for the kill, if I recall," the senator said with a small smile.

Sharyn guessed from the senator's tone that those were qualities he found appealing. She sipped at her ice water and hoped they were planning on leaving soon. She needed to go to bed and close her eyes.

"Wasn't that your deputy, David someone-or-other, I saw getting out of Julia Richmond's car this afternoon?" Caison asked her with a sly smile. "He's made short work of gaining her notice. Of course, she's a young, beautiful, rich widow now."

"That was the Porsche, wasn't it?" Kristie asked innocently.

"And isn't that Nick Thomopolis over there at that table?" Faye asked, waving at him. "He's such a handsome man, isn't he, Sharyn? Nick! Oh, Nick!"

SEVEN

NICK WALKED OVER TO their table with a gorgeous blonde on his arm. She was wearing a stunning red dress that made Sharyn writhe just looking at it. There wasn't a bulge or a curve out of place. Sharyn rested her arms protectively across her chest.

"Faye," Nick acknowledged her. "It's nice to see you."

"You, too," Faye greeted him. "And who's this?"

"A friend from New York. Tigre Adams. Tigre, this is Faye Howard, Senator Caison Talbot, Kristin Howard, and Sheriff Sharyn Howard."

"So you're Sharyn Howard," Tigre said at once, her eyes slicing and dicing Sharyn's plain blue sweater, black skirt, and makeup-less face.

Sharyn hid behind a sip of water. "Hello, Nick. Nice to meet you, Tigre."

Nick glanced at Sharyn's face. "I heard you were hurt."

"Not seriously," she countered with a small laugh. "Otherwise I wouldn't be here, would I?"

"So, Nick, another murder to solve," Caison said with a frown. "You must be busy."

"I have a new assistant, thanks to Sharyn, otherwise I wouldn't be here."

"Tigre, that's a great dress! Bet you didn't get that off the rack," Kristie said.

"As a matter of fact, I got it because I modeled for a friend of mine. It was a gift," the woman replied.

"Why don't you join us?" Faye suggested. "We're about to have some brandy."

Nick looked at Sharyn. "All right, thanks."

Sharyn knew she couldn't tolerate brandy at that moment, and the pain in her head was getting worse. She wasn't sure she could tolerate being at the same table with Nick and Tigre, although it certainly didn't matter to her who Nick dated. He was probably throwing Tigre in her face because she'd asked him about dating Julia Richmond. She wondered briefly what had happened to his preference for redheads. On the other hand, she guessed, looking at Tigre, the woman could have been a redhead last week.

"I really have to go," Sharyn said suddenly. She stood up and knocked over what was left in her glass. Water spilled on the table and rolled to the floor.

"My daughter, the graceful one," Faye Howard remarked caustically.

Kristie handed Sharyn an extra napkin and Sharyn cleaned up the mess on the table.

"Are you okay?" she asked her older sister. "You don't look so good."

"Thanks," Sharyn said quietly. "I'll be fine. I just remembered something I have to do at the office. Nice meeting you, Tigre. Sorry about dinner, Mom. Senator, Nick."

Sharyn marched out of the restaurant, feeling tears welling in her eyes. It was because she was hurt and sick and she needed to be in bed, she told herself. She got out to the front of the restaurant, then remembered that she'd taken a taxi because the doctor had begged her not to drive for at least twenty-four hours. She started to go back in and ask the host to call a taxi for her and ran directly into Nick.

"What now?" she demanded, moving back from him at once. "Another tirade? Another way to make me look stupid? Did I forget to call a taxi? Yes, I did. I'm used to driving. Am I graceful as a gazelle, like my mother and sister? No, I'm not. My head hurts and I'm sick to my stomach. Should I be here? No, I probably shouldn't be but I had this stupid idea that they wanted me to be here, so here I am!"

"Well," Nick drawled slowly. "At least you got the part right that you shouldn't be here and you didn't drive. I give you credit for that."

Sharyn paused and stared at him. "What do you want, Nick?"

He sighed and took her arm. "Probably not what you think, Sharyn. Right now, I want to give you a ride home."

"Why?" she demanded, even though she was walking out to his car with him.

"Because your head hurts and you're sick to your stomach. Head injuries are like that, you know. That's why you're supposed to lie down, preferably in bed, and take it easy for a while."

He helped her into the passenger side of his black Cadillac, then got behind the wheel. "Are you all right? You don't need a paper bag or anything? Because I just had this cleaned out last week."

She sniffed. "I'm okay for now."

"Good." He started the engine. "So, what happened?"

"I was going to check out the cemetery at the boys' school and someone hit me in the head."

He stopped and looked at her. "He could've killed you."

"Obviously he didn't need to," she replied lightly. "He just stopped me from finding whatever it was in the cemetery."

"But wasn't the little boy supposed to be buried on the hill by the bridge?"

"He was," she agreed. "But we checked out

there, and there was no freshly opened ground that we could find. I sent Lennie and Jeremy back with Ed so they wouldn't clock in any overtime after the storm."

"Jeremy was there?"

"I would've called you but you were still in class."

"Surely even Jeremy can make out a place where a body has decayed," he admitted sourly. "He's a big help. Except that I have to go back over most of his stuff."

"You picked him out," she reminded him.

"I know. You didn't fire David. So those remains must've been buried in the cemetery, then."

"And the person who killed Beau must have known that he dropped something at the site where he dug up the bones. He must have been following Beau around and that's how he knew to find him at the station that night."

"He dropped something," Nick ruminated as he drove down the dark street. "Or Beau dropped something that he didn't want us to find." He brought the car to a screeching halt in the empty street.

"What's wrong?" she wondered aloud, watching him as he made a turn in the street.

"It might be nothing but there's something I have to look at."

"Something that might have dropped?"

He nodded. "Can you hold on a few minutes?"

"Kristie said I can do anything for Diamond Springs," she quoted briefly.

They got out at the hospital and went into the basement where the morgue was located. Nick had an office there that he shared with Jeremy, leased by the county for the medical examiner. Sharyn sat down on the sofa that Nick was always describing as his sleeping place, and Nick started through some photographs.

"What are you looking for?" she asked after a few minutes.

"I'm not sure," he explained a few minutes later. "There was something that bothered me about the remains. It's there but right at the edge of... Wait, there it is! I knew I remembered seeing it! There's a place on the left wrist. It looks like something must have been there when the body was decomposing because it eventually left a mark against the bone. That probably meant metal, like a name bracelet or a watch. There was nothing like that with the remains. Beau must have dropped it when he picked them up and the killer knew about it. He probably went back for it and there you were, snooping around."

Nick studied the discolored area in the picture on the left radius. "This might prove the theory about Judge Hamilton. It's hard to believe he could be involved in all of this but if the boy's remains were part of the issue, it seems to be him for sure. And Sheriff Sharyn Howard solves another dastardly deed in Diamond Springs!"

He looked up from the photo. Sharyn was asleep on the sofa. He sighed. It was just as well, he decided, getting up from his chair and going to stand at her side. She shouldn't have been alone with a head injury. Who knew when her mother and sister would make it home? And would they know what to look for if there was a problem?

He put her feet up on the sofa and spread her long skirt down around her ankles, easing off her shoes. She never opened her eyes. He pulled up the old wool blanket he still had from his days in the military. She stirred a little but didn't open her eyes. He crouched down next to her and studied her freckled face, trying to imagine what she would look like in ten years when she was his age. Would she be married and have children? Would she still be the sheriff of Diamond Springs?

He touched a soft curl, the color of a new penny, that was resting near her cheek. She smiled a little in her sleep. He kissed her cheek and whispered, "Good night, Sharyn." Then he turned off the light and leaned back in the old black chair behind his desk. He left the photos out to show her in the morning then went to sleep looking at her.

Sharyn woke up early in the morning. She looked around her and almost fell off the sofa. Where was she?

She remembered coming back to the morgue with Nick to look at something. Photos. She realized that she must have fallen asleep while he was looking at the pictures. She remembered him saying something about the killer following Beau Richmond and wanting to take something that Beau had dropped from the remains.

She got up quietly and looked at Nick, sleeping in the chair. His dark face was almost angelic in sleep, especially in the dim light from the hospital corridor. She glanced at the pictures then put on her shoes. She was going to have to go and see Judge Hamilton one more time.

By the time she had showered and dressed in her uniform at home, she was feeling human again. Her head didn't hurt unless she moved it too quickly and she didn't feel like crying. That was an important aspect to her well-being because Michaelson was waiting for her when she got to the office.

"I already have a search warrant for his office and his home," he told her without bothering to explain.

"Good morning to you, too," she said shortly. "I take it you've decided to stop looking out for your career and have me arrest Judge Hamilton?"

"We can't ignore the evidence, Sheriff," he told

JOYCE & JIM LAVENE 163

her with a sincerity that she found astonishing and totally unbelievable. "It's not a matter of careers but a matter of protecting the citizens of Diamond Springs. Obviously, he hit you in the head yesterday to keep you from finding something incriminating in the cemetery. What else would he do to protect himself?"

Sharyn stared at him. "You've already heard about the photos, haven't you?"

Michaelson preened. "I try to keep up with the investigation."

"I don't believe—"

"It doesn't matter what you believe," Michaelson assured her bluntly. "What matters is that Judge Hamilton had motive, opportunity, and no real alibi for the night he killed Beau Richmond. I'm the assistant district attorney, Sheriff. I'm standing here with an arrest warrant and a search warrant for Judge Hamilton's home and office. The DA wants this wrapped up quickly. It's going to be embarrassing enough when a district court judge is arrested for murder."

"But a nice job opening, huh?" Sharyn debated quietly.

Michaelson glared at her. "Just do your job, Sheriff, and I'll do mine." He walked out of the building and didn't look back.

Sharyn knew that he was right. At least about

picking up Judge Hamilton. She didn't believe Walter Hamilton had sneaked into their office the night of the blizzard and murdered Beau Richmond any more than she believed that he had knocked her in the head at the school cemetery, but she couldn't prove that to Michaelson.

She looked around her. Ed and Joe were there but there was no sign of Lennie or Ernie. "Trudy, have you heard from Ernie this morning?"

"Not yet," Trudy told her. "But he's been coming in late."

"Call David for me," Sharyn said quietly. "Tell him that I need to see him. Ed, I guess you'll have to hold the fort until Ernie or Lennie come in. Joe, you're with me."

"Are you gonna have to suspend him, Sheriff?" Ed asked with a worried frown. "Not that he's not such an idiot that he doesn't deserve it."

"I'm reprimanding him right now," she confided. "It's just a formality, saying that he was wrong. I hope it ends there. If not, I don't know what will happen, Ed."

"I know you've done what you could for him," his uncle observed. "Thanks, Sheriff."

She nodded and put on her hat. Outside, the ADA had called a press conference on the sunlit stairs of the courthouse building. Reporters were lined up to hear about the sheriff's office arresting someone for the murder of Beau Richmond. Sharyn was shocked when he gave the press the judge's name. Judge Hamilton could hear about his arrest for murder before Sharyn could get there to do it!

Julia Richmond's sleek Porsche squealed up to the curb in front of them and David climbed out of the interior. He had shaved his mustache and was wearing a pair of sunglasses that rested on his nose as he looked at her.

"Sheriff."

"David."

"I heard you put out a call for me?"

"That's right," Sharyn said with a smile. "But not right here next to Michaelson's circus. Let's just hope they don't pick up on you being here with *her* at all."

"We're in love," David stated brightly. "We have nothing to hide."

But it was too late for that. A member of the press with sharp eyes caught sight of the deputy getting out of Julia Richmond's car. It only took a moment for the rest of the pack to smell blood.

"He's done this to himself," Sharyn told Joe sharply. "Let's get out of here."

The press were all over the Porsche, making it impossible for David and Julia to pull away from the curb. Sharyn saw Ed coming out of the station, then Joe pulled the squad car around the corner.

"That boy doesn't have the sense he was born

with, Sheriff," Joe grumbled with a shake of his head. "I understand Ed wanting the best for him, but he's an idiot! We all know you should have fired him for what he did that night."

"Beau wasn't in custody," Sharyn said slowly. "He wasn't our prisoner so we weren't technically protecting him. There was no way to know he was a threat to his own life or that someone else might want to kill him. I don't blame David entirely. The circumstances were as much to blame."

Joe shook his head and grinned. "You are so much like your daddy! I can sit here and imagine him saying the same thing! He was the fairest man I've ever known. You're just like him."

"Thanks, Joe. That means a lot to me."

"He would have been proud of the way you've done things. I wasn't sure at first, you know—"

"I know."

"But we all think the world of you, Sheriff. I just wanted you to know that."

"Thanks, Joe. I think the world of all of you, too."

They crossed the temporary bridge that was keeping the main road together after the flooding from the snow. The main bridge was out over the creek that roared down from the mountains.

"When did this bridge go out after the storm?" she asked, thinking quickly.

"I'm not sure," Joe responded, picking up her idea at once. "I'll call in and see if anyone knows."

Three bridges in the area had gone out that night. All the residents in the communities beyond them had been stranded until the temporary bridges had been set up. It wasn't an uncommon occurrence since they were in the flood path of three rivers that came together at the base of the Uwharries. Fortunately, the Army Corps of Engineers had helped them out with durable evacuation bridges that could be used until the bridges could be repaired. The crossings were small, but when the rivers were raging, no one could cross without the bridge.

"Trudy says the best anyone can tell, the bridge was out here at eleven," Joe said after talking to the office. "So, Judge Hamilton couldn't have killed Beau."

"It still hinges on his wife's word that he was home," Sharyn reminded him. "Even if he didn't try to go out until the evacuation bridge was in place the next day, unless someone saw him here, his alibi is still weak."

Joe made a face. "I think Ed was right. We should shoot Michaelson."

Sharyn laughed. "The evidence is circumstantial. I know Judge Hamilton didn't sneak into the office and kill Beau! He might know where the key is kept and he might have had motive and opportunity, but that doesn't make him a killer."

"So, who do you think did it?"

"I don't know, Joe. There are a few things going on here that don't make sense yet. Until they do, we won't understand why Beau was murdered."

"Michaelson doesn't believe those attacks on the judge's life were real?"

"They weren't exactly eye-catching. Jeremy's report said that it was natural aging of the cement around the statue that caused it to fall. He said they couldn't find any sign that it had been chipped away. The mechanic that Ernie talked to about the judge's brakes was pretty much the same about that situation. It might have been human error. It could have been something else. Not very convincing."

Joe shrugged. "I guess we have to hope if there is another killer that he doesn't decide to get convincing suddenly and we lose the judge, too."

"The forensics report points to Judge Hamilton being involved with Beau's death. Someone attacked me in the school cemetery and the motive could have been something left behind that Nick thinks could be a bracelet or watch. That leads to the judge again, since he admits he and Beau did something with that boy forty years ago. Who else has any reason to cover it up?"

"No one that we know of," Joe agreed. "But the judge just doesn't seem the type, you know?"

"I know." Sharyn saw the first plume of smoke from the road above the trees. It filled her with foreboding.

"Is that smoke coming from the judge's house?" Joe wondered.

"Looks like it," she decided. "Step on it, Joe."

They made the last turn into the Hamiltons' drive and saw the black smoke billowing out of the house. Only the right side and the garage seemed to be involved at that moment.

"Call it in," she said to Joe as he stopped the car sharply away from the house. "I'm going in."

"Sheriff!"

Sharyn *knew* that Judge Hamilton was in that smoldering house. The killer had decided to stop playing around and make the judge's death a reality. Smoke was coming, thick and white, from the center of the house. The garage door was partially open and black smoke was spewing out.

"Oh, Walter!" his wife said, pulling up in the drive behind them and jumping out of her car. "Oh, no!!"

"Stay back," Sharyn heard Joe tell the woman. "The fire department is on the way."

"Sheriff, Walter's in there! I just went to the pharmacy for a prescription. I was only gone a short time! I left him sleeping! Oh, Walter!"

Sharyn entered through the back of the house. She could see where the lock had been broken and the door was left open. She wanted to believe that the fire department would make it in time to save the judge, but the same instinct that told her the judge was in the house told her that it wouldn't happen that way. The killer was clever. He wouldn't have given the judge that much time.

The smoke was thick but she got down on her knees and crawled across the floor. Mrs. Hamilton had said that she left her husband sleeping but there was no sign of him in the bedroom. The upstairs rooms were rapidly filling with smoke, although there was no sign of fire there. Sheets and blankets were thrown everywhere. The lamp on the bedside table was on the floor. There had been a struggle. She called Judge Hamilton repeatedly but there was no response.

Sharyn knew she didn't have a lot of time. She thought about the garage door being partially open and went back downstairs. While it was true that his wife was out, her only lead was the door that was left ajar. In an otherwise flawless setting, it rankled her nerves. She couldn't see anything actually on fire in the house until she got to the kitchen. The fire seemed to be coming from the garage where it met the kitchen wall. Coughing a little, she grabbed a towel and wet it, then pressed it across her nose and mouth.

Opening the door from the kitchen to the garage, she lay flat against the cool tile on the floor and looked out into the smoke-filled garage. There was a burgundy Lincoln parked inside. The judge's car. The garage was in flames but the Lincoln was only smoldering. The gas cap was open on the car. But there was no sign of the judge. It smelled strongly of gasoline, despite the heavy scent of smoke. She could hear things popping and exploding everywhere around her. It was only a matter of time before the fire reached the car and it exploded. Already, tiny flames danced on the hood and trunk.

Could the judge be in the car? She called his name again but there was no response. She wasn't sure she could have heard anything less than an active shout in the rush of the fire and the sounds of destruction around her anyway. She looked at the car again. If she tried that route, it would be her final attempt at saving the man's life. The house was going up too quickly to have any time to come back.

Sharyn looked at the garage floor. The concrete was alive with every kind of tool and device as well as broken glass and live wires but she could see a path where someone had dragged something across it. That decided it for her. She would have to stay low and try to reach the judge to get him out.

If the pattern played out and he was either dead or unconscious from a blow to the back of the head, she knew it was going to be more difficult. The judge was a big man. She wasn't sure if she could carry him to safety. Unfortunately, she didn't have much time to plan what she could do to get them both out of there. Any plan could lead to both their deaths.

But she didn't plan on dying that day. She had way too much to do. Without thinking any further about what to do, she plunged into the garage. She tried to keep her head low but the heat and smoke were intense. She only had a few moments to get out of there and take the judge with her. She didn't have time to check on him, to be sure that he was in the car. She had to trust her instincts. They centered around the disarray in the garage. The judge or his wife wouldn't have left the place that way, and it looked as if someone could have dragged him there.

Saying a small prayer, she climbed into the Lincoln. She was coughing violently. She threw aside the towel that had dried in her hands from the heat and pulled the door closed. It wasn't much respite from the fire but it was better than nothing. Quickly, she forced stinging eyes to look above the sun visor. There were no keys waiting there. Frantic now as the smoke began to seep into the car and the interior temperature began to rise, she flailed on the floor beneath the mat. Smoke was rising from the floor-boards, almost obscuring her vision.

She searched for something to open the ignition so she could hot-wire the car when a jangle of keys made her heart leap. Thank goodness for the eighty percent of people who kept their keys in those places! But the smoke and her own tearing eyes were making it impossible to find their resting place. She shuffled her feet and heard them again. She felt the bulge in the mat and stepped on it to keep it in place.

With lungs bursting for fresh air, she managed to put the key into the ignition. She started the car quickly, gunning the engine and hoping that there was no one in the drive outside the garage door. Five firefighters jumped aside in surprise when they saw the smoking Lincoln crash through the door and continue into the yard. They aimed their hoses at the car, putting out the smoldering paint that had just caught fire, as well as the smoking tires.

Sharyn opened the door, only to be pushed back into the smoke-filled interior by the force of the water. Gasping for air and finding her nose and mouth filled with water, she coughed violently and heard people yelling. The fires doused on the car, the firemen turned the hoses away and she stumbled from the car, throwing herself on the cool green grass. She took in huge gulps of fresh air and tried to get to her feet.

"Sheriff! Come over this way," Joe was saying, pulling at her arm.

"Judge," she wheezed. "Trunk."

She couldn't see where she was going. Her eyes were filled with soot that was making vision impossible. Joe led her to an ambulance where they gave her oxygen while he went to help the paramedics take Judge Hamilton from the trunk of his car. Two paramedics were on the ground with him, trying to revive him.

Sharyn closed her eyes after the paramedic put drops in her eyes to help with the smoke damage. She breathed in the oxygen her lungs were greedily demanding and hoped that the judge was still alive. She'd been right and she'd managed to get him out of the burning garage, but she didn't know if it was in time.

"Are you all right, Sheriff?" the paramedic asked.

"I'm fine," she managed to gasp out.

"Keep that mask on your face. I'm going to help with the judge."

"Is he alive?" Ellen Hamilton was demanding loudly. "Walter! Walter, can you hear me?"

Something exploded violently in the house. Sharyn tried to see but her vision was too blurry. Someone yelled that the natural gas was off. Mrs. Hamilton was crying. There was the sound of breaking glass coming from the house and another siren approaching from the drive.

"He's alive," Joe told her breathlessly. "Ernie and Ed are on their way here."

She opened her eyes and squinted at his worried face. "Good."

"How about you?" he wondered. "Are you okay?"

"I will be," she responded, taking a blanket from him.

"They said the house is gone," he explained. "The fire just burned too hot, too fast. You're lucky the two of you got out alive. Fire chief is furious. He says he's gonna report you to the commissioners. Sheriff's department is supposed to stay out until the fire department gets there."

She nodded.

"But the Hamiltons might want to give you a medal," he continued. "They wouldn't have been here in time to find him. How'd you know where to look?"

"I didn't," she answered shortly. "Not for sure. Lucky guess."

"You got enough of those to go around!" He smiled at her.

"I know." She smiled back.

"But you're black as pitch," he commented.

She glanced at him and saw soot all over him as well. "You, too."

He laughed. "Think the ADA will take the judge's word for it that someone wants to kill him?"

"I hope so." She felt the ache in her chest start to ease. "The question is, who?"

Ed and Ernie arrived a minute later and ran from the car to where Joe and Sharyn were sitting in the back of an ambulance.

"Is she okay?" Ernie asked at once.

"I'm fine," Sharyn answered for herself. "Just got some smoke."

"If that don't beat all," Ernie remarked, taking off his hat and hitting his leg with it. "I suppose you waltzed in there and rescued the judge?"

Ed smiled. "You know she did."

"Sheriff?" Ellen Hamilton called.

The deputies surrounding her moved aside and the soot-covered woman came closer.

"Are you all right, Sheriff?" she asked.

"I'm all right, Mrs. Hamilton."

"I—I don't know how to thank you. They're taking Walter to the hospital. He's alive. I don't know how long." She broke down and Ed offered her a clean white handkerchief.

"I'm sorry, Mrs. Hamilton," Sharyn said.

"I know now," Ellen told her with a bitter grimace. "I know about the whole thing. Walter told me. He also told me that he gave Beau twenty-five-thousand dollars to stop acting crazy and trying to ruin both their lives. I—I don't know what he was thinking, Sheriff."

"He was trying to save a lifetime of good that was about to be ruined by a moment of bad from forty years ago," Sharyn excused him. "I think it's a reasonable trade-off."

"Just now," Ellen told her, "he was muttering that boy's name over and over. I don't know if he's finally convinced himself that they did kill the boy or that he's responsible. I don't know, Sheriff."

"Why don't you go on with your husband now?" Ernie said to the distraught woman. "He's going to need you."

Ellen smiled. "I know. For the first time in his life, he's going to need me. And I can't help him." She looked at Sharyn. "I just wanted you to know about the money, Sheriff. I hope you'll be all right."

"I'll be fine," Sharyn repeated. "Take care of your husband, Mrs. Hamilton."

"I'll stay with the sheriff until she's ready to go," Ernie decided. He was the senior officer under Sharyn, and after her, they looked to him for what to do.

Ed nodded. "I'll drive back with Joe. What do you want us to do?"

"Take a look at that cemetery at the school,"

Sharyn told them. "Be careful in case whoever did this is still looking for what was dropped. If you find anything, call Nick or Jeremy and let them take a team up there."

"Okay," Ed agreed. "You take it easy, Sheriff."

Joe shook his head. "And no more running into burning houses! You trying to get a medal or something?"

She laughed. "See you back at the office. Be careful. There's someone out there, besides the judge, who doesn't want us to find out what's going on."

EIGHT

THE PARAMEDIC RELEASED Sharyn twenty minutes later. He told her to come to the hospital if she had any other problems breathing. Sharyn thanked him, then climbed into the squad car with Ernie driving.

"Glad it wasn't more serious," Ernie remarked as they started out. "You could've been killed."

"I hope the judge makes it," she answered. "He might be able to tell us who's responsible. I could tell he struggled with whoever put him in the trunk of his car. He had to see his face."

"If he can remember after that hit on the head and the smoke inhalation," Ernie countered.

"That's true," she agreed. "We should have taken those first two threats more seriously."

Ernie shrugged his thin shoulders. "How could we? They didn't look like much of anything."

"I don't know," she admitted. "I've known from the beginning that the judge didn't sneak in here Sunday night and kill Beau Richmond. Can you imagine this man sneaking anywhere?"

"Nobody is all that they seem, Sheriff," he corrected. He pulled the car off on the side of the road before they reached the temporary bridge that crossed the river. "I have to talk to you, Sharyn. And it's not gonna be something you want to hear."

She sat back in her seat and looked at the man she'd grown up with in her house and her life. Ernie was her father's best friend as well as his right hand in the sheriff's office. When she'd taken over, she'd continued the tradition. They weren't as close as he had been with her father. There was always an age and respect barrier between them. Ernie insisted on according her the respect he felt she deserved as the sheriff. She insisted on according him the respect she felt he had earned being there for all of them after her father had been killed.

She had been so happy for him when he found Annie again, but then his life had fallen apart. Hadn't she known for weeks that it was something more than that? Hadn't she wanted to ask, but that barrier kept her silent?

"You called me Sharyn," she pointed out. "It must be serious."

He smiled in a worried, weary way. "I've watched you grow up. You know that. I saw you take your first steps. I've wanted to make sure there wasn't anything that people could criticize between us when you took your daddy's place. I've tried not to be too familiar or to take advantage of our relationship."

He looked at her squarely. "But now, I'm about to do just that."

Sharyn's heart was pounding and her mouth felt dry. Either feeling, she knew, she could attribute to running into a smoke-filled house and breathing oxygen afterward, but she knew that this was fear. She'd felt it before, lots of times. Sometimes it seemed as if it was a part of her life since her father died, like breathing and eating. She didn't remember it before that day. But she knew it would always be there, whether she was sheriff or not.

"What is it, Ernie?"

He took a deep breath and looked away from her again. "I was there, Sharyn."

She studied his averted face. "Where?"

"At Jefferson. Forty years ago." He stopped and squirmed in his seat. "I don't know how to tell you this. I've never told anyone this before. The three of us never even talked about it until two month ago."

Sharyn felt the breath leave her body. "You helped them kill Michael Smith?"

Ernie gripped the steering wheel until his knuckles turned white. "I don't know if I can explain. I was eight at the time. My daddy was gone. I stole something and wouldn't go to school. They told my mother I could avoid going to jail with the adults if I went to Jefferson."

"But Ernie—"

"Please let me finish," he asked. "I have to say all of this and it's like pulling teeth."

"Sorry."

He smiled at her quickly, that Ernie half-smile she'd known since she was a child.

"I went to the school but it wasn't like a school. It was a bunch of mean boys all locked up together. They treated us like mules, working us all day, barely feeding us. I can't believe jail would've been worse. I watched boys keel over in the heat and saw the men drag them away. Some of them, I never saw again. But I did see new graves in the cemetery."

He leaned his head against the window. "I was little for my age, scrawny as a stick. The minute I walked in there, the bigger boys began to pick on me. At night, they'd come and drag you out of your bed and make you walk naked while they beat you. They did everything you can imagine and then some. It was a nightmare. I knew Beau and Walt, even though they were a lot older. I worked on our friendship, did things for them they didn't want to do, just to get them to protect me. They were as mean or meaner than the rest. Pretty soon, nobody bothered me anymore. I stole food for them and found out secrets. I would've done anything to keep them on my side. Things were going okay. Then Michael Smith was put in our building."

Sharyn put her head back against the seat. She was

like Ernie's family and she was the sheriff, hearing a terrible confession. She didn't want to be there. She didn't want to hear these things about this man.

"Michael was small and he couldn't talk right. He couldn't understand what was going on. I tried to get him to find someone to protect him but he couldn't think straight or something. They beat him and humiliated him. He was so simpleminded that he didn't seem to understand what was happening. That made it even more fun for them. I tried to help him but I had to be careful of my own neck. Walt and Beau picked on him, too."

Ernie gazed out the window. "That night, Walt told me he was gonna have some fun with Michael. Beau and he were gonna take Michael down to where they were building the bridge to the chapel. They were gonna rough him up and make him spend the night down there. They wanted me to go with them. We got Michael and walked down to the bridge. He was crying because they had slapped him around some. His mouth was bleeding. They made him drink some moonshine they made back in one of the barns. They were already lit up with it."

Sharyn took in a deep breath at the same time as Ernie.

"I didn't see who actually hit him in the head. It was dark except for the moon. The first I knew, he was rolling down the hill and then he didn't move.

Beau laughed and Walt said I should go and get him so they could tell him that he was gonna have to spend the night out there. I slipped down after him but he didn't move. I felt his chest but I couldn't feel any heartbeat. He wasn't breathing. I told them we should go and get the doc or at least leave him in the infirmary, but they didn't want to hear it. They dug out a little spot right there where he was and threw some leaves over him. I expected them to find him the next day but no one was surprised when they didn't say anything about it. Boys disappeared all the time."

"Oh, Ernie."

He buried his face in his hands. "I've lived with it every day of my life for forty years. It's part of why I became a deputy. When they shut down that place, I was happy. Anything was better than that."

"Why didn't Beau name you in his confession?"

"Two weeks ago, Beau called me and asked me if I remembered Michael. I told him I did. He told me that Michael's ghost had visited him and wanted him to confess. He told me that Walt had already told him to keep his mouth shut, even gave him some money, but he was gonna have to talk to get the ghost away from him. He said the ghost didn't blame me because I didn't really do anything."

Sharyn shuddered with the knowledge. "Why didn't you tell me right away?"

"Even after we found Beau dead, I prayed it would

go away again. I knew what it would mean. We all knew what it would mean."

Sharyn's mind was racing along the lines it was supposed to, and she didn't like the outcome. Ernie's confession gave him as much motive and access to kill Beau as the judge. But it was worse than that. Hadn't he been with the judge minutes before the statue had fallen from the courthouse? Hadn't he been the one to find her at the cemetery after she was attacked?

"Where were you this morning, Ernie?"

"I was down at the lake, trying to get my thoughts together."

"Did anyone see you?"

"No. I was alone."

Sharyn searched his face. She saw torment and anguish in his eyes. "I'm sorry. You knew I'd have to ask."

"I know," he whispered. "I know you have to suspend me. I know this is gonna make you look bad, and I'm sorry."

"Ernie, I'm more worried about you from here. Michaelson is going to look at this and see what both of us see right now. Motive, opportunity, and access. You don't have an alibi for this morning. You were missing when the statue fell on the judge. You were off by yourself when the fire started at the judge's house and he was attacked. You've been acting strangely for a while. Your records are going to show that you've come in late and left early a lot."

"Just answer me one question, Sheriff, and I don't care much after that what Michaelson or anybody else thinks. Do you think I killed Beau and attacked the judge? Do you think I attacked *you?*"

Her gaze never wavered. "Never. But it does look bad for you."

He nodded. "I know. But as long as you don't think—" He turned his head to the side away from her intent gaze.

"I have to suspend you, Ernie."

"You should arrest me. We both know that."

"But right now, Michaelson is working on the judge being the culprit. Arresting you wouldn't do any good. We have to find out who's responsible. When we get to the station, I want you to call Annie and I don't want you to leave her sight again until this is over. In fact, the more people you're with the better. We both know you didn't do any of this. We have to give the real killer a chance to hang himself."

"If you lock me up, it would be the perfect alibi," he reminded her.

"Unless Judge Hamilton dies and the killer is satisfied. If nothing else happens, it would all point to you."

"I didn't do it."

"I don't think so. But Michaelson will."

They reached the office. Sharyn's mind was teeming with plans to save Ernie. Was it really possible that all of this revolved around Michael Smith's death? If so, was it a long-lost relative who knew the truth and wanted revenge?

"Call Annie," Sharyn said again to Ernie. "Check out for the day. Don't say anything to anyone. I don't know how information is reaching Michaelson but I don't want him to know about your suspension yet. It might give us the day to sort through everything."

Ernie nodded. "Thanks, Sheriff."

Sharyn went to the locker room and changed her wet, sooty uniform and washed up. Then she went to her office. Trudy followed her in and closed the door.

"Michaelson was here earlier looking for you. He's rescinded the arrest warrant for the judge. Ed and Joe found the place where the bones were snatched in the Jefferson cemetery. They have Jeremy and a team from the college out there now."

"Thanks, Trudy."

Trudy laughed. "Ed and Joe expect to be cleaned up over there and back at the office in a little while. Nick called. He's on his way over to see you." She rolled her eyes and pursed her lips.

"What?" Sharyn asked.

"Nick spends a lot of time with you, Sheriff."

"He works with me, Trudy."

"He worked with your daddy, too," Trudy said with a sparkle in her blue eyes. "But he never spent so much time with him!"

Sharyn shook her head. "Go back to work, Trudy."

Trudy laughed, then left the office.

Sharyn put down her pen and stared thoughtfully across the room. Ernie was in trouble. Terrible trouble. She wasn't sure if she could help him unless they could find the person responsible. She called Lennie, wondering how much she could tell him without telling him everything. A few weeks ago, she thought she could trust anyone in her office. Now she knew better. She didn't need this information leaked to Michaelson yet. She needed time to find the real killer.

Nick opened the office door and came in as usual, without knocking. Sharyn sat back in her chair and looked at him, wondering if she could trust him.

"'Morning. You look better," he said, searching her face with a jaundiced eye. "I wish I felt that good. Sleeping in that chair is like having someone saw off part of your back."

"About that," she ventured carefully.

He sat down and shuffled his briefcase around on his lap. "Yes?"

"I appreciate your help last night. I said some stupid things and I should've stayed home."

"Or in the hospital. I hear you survived running into a burning house this morning already."

"Don't start."

"You're a good sheriff," he said, his black eyes pinning her to her seat. "But you take unnecessary chances. You should've waited for the fire department."

"Judge Hamilton would be dead, then," she countered fiercely. "I *know* what I'm doing."

Nick raised his hands in frustration. "Talking to you is like— Never mind." He opened up his briefcase. "I have a few more pieces of the puzzle for you. I know you'll need them now since the judge is obviously out of the suspect picture."

Sharyn looked at the reports he gave her. "You found Michael Smith's dental records?"

"Yep. And the remains aren't his."

"What?"

"Take a look," he said, moving in next to her. "These are some old records but they were done right after Michael Smith got to the school. Apparently, he had really bad teeth and they had started fixing them for him. There wasn't a cavity in this set of teeth. They were perfect."

Sharyn looked at him. "So, the skeleton Beau dug up wasn't the boy he and Walt said they killed?"

"Not if he was Michael Smith."

"But Beau must have thought it was the boy," she mused over the grainy records.

"Somebody else must've thought so, too, or they

wouldn't have cared if you were out there looking around."

Sharyn put the records down on her desk. "I think it must be the head injury. None of this makes any sense."

"Well, then, you're going to love this," he said, going back to his seat. "I took a look at the courthouse roof today and Jeremy was wrong again. I don't know where that man keeps his brains! That statue was practically sawed off its base. There was no loose concrete but the break was clean. Concrete never breaks cleanly by itself."

"Can you put out the dental records on the Internet for the skeleton that we have?" Sharyn asked.

"Done. Could be a while before we find the match, though."

"I know," Sharyn said, wishing she thought they had a while to play with. "What are you going to do about Jeremy?"

Nick shrugged. "Nothing. He means well. He's willing to take on all the stuff I don't want to do. He doesn't mind getting up early in the morning or crawling around in the dirt. I think he'll learn. He does a pretty good autopsy. He just doesn't have much practical experience."

"I guess he's yours to deal with," Sharyn added quickly. "It's your problem if he makes a mistake you don't catch."

There was a knock at the door. Jeremy entered along with Lennie, Ed, and Joe. At that moment, when she looked at all of them together, Sharyn knew her informer had to be Jeremy or Lennie. The other men, even Trudy, had been there for too long. They weren't motivated by political goals, like Lennie, or trying to fit in, like Jeremy. She wanted to know, though, and she had a plan to find out.

"I'm glad to see all of you," she told them. "How did the dig go?"

"We found a gravesite, off by itself. Kind of messed up. No headstone," Ed told her. "There were some shreds of clothing and some other stuff. Jeremy can tell you more."

Jeremy smiled and stepped close to Sharyn's big desk. "I took some earth samples and some of the material and bone fragments." He held up one of the big plastic bags. "I think this was the spot, Sheriff. We should know more shortly."

Sharyn glanced at the bag then smiled at the man. "Good job, Jeremy. I appreciate you being willing to go out there."

"No problem, Sheriff," he told her, obviously pleased by her response.

"Ed, if you and Joe would like to get cleaned up, I need to see you in about half an hour in the conference room. Thanks for the information, Nick. Let me know if you hear anything else about the missing child."

"Missing child?" Jeremy wondered.

"The dental records don't match the bones," Nick explained baldly. "We're looking for another kid."

"What about Michael Smith?" Jeremy wondered.

"We don't know yet," Sharyn answered. "We might never find his body."

"Pretty good bet the road went right over it," Ed replied.

"How's the judge doing?" Joe asked.

"Last I heard, he was in a coma," Sharyn told them. "The doctors aren't very hopeful."

"I guess those other attempts were real after all," Joe said.

"Not the statue from the roof," Jeremy told him.

"I'm afraid we'll have to disagree on that," Nick objected.

"I examined the area. There were no cement chips!" Jeremy told him indignantly.

"Let's go for a walk, Jeremy," Nick suggested, putting his arm around the other man's shoulders. "We need to have a talk."

Lennie glanced around the office. "I guess that leaves me."

Sharyn gave him the file on Michael Smith. "I need to know if there's anyone still alive that can help us with this. Relatives, I guess. He lived around here. There might be someone left who knew him."

Lennie nodded. "We're looking for a new killer?"

"We're looking for something else about Michael Smith," she answered flatly. "If he died, the family must've been informed. Find me some relatives."

Lennie glanced around. "Where's Ernie?"

"He's off for the day again." Sharyn sighed. "I don't know what's up with him."

"He's in love," Lennie told her with a smile.

"Not in this office," she told him briefly. "Find me Michael Smith's family."

Ed and Joe met her in the conference room. They knew something was wrong when she closed the door and sat down at the table with them.

"Don't you want to wait for Ernie?" Ed asked pointedly. Until recently, Ernie was always with the sheriff. He'd believed in her from the beginning. He'd helped convince the rest of them that she could do the job.

"This is about Ernie," she told them. "I've suspended him from the sheriff's department."

Joe winced and Ed sat back in his chair with a frown on his face.

"What happened, Sheriff?" Joe demanded. "How could it be that bad?"

"Is Michaelson behind this?" Ed questioned closely. "Couldn't we appeal?"

"I suspended Ernie," she explained painfully. "It's difficult to explain, but Ernie is a suspect in this murder investigation."

"Ernie?" Joe shook his head. "I've known him all my life. No way Ernie murdered anybody!"

"It's Michaelson," Ed concluded with a grim smile.

"It's not Michaelson," she defended. "But we're in here without Lennie because of Michaelson." She explained what Ernie had confessed to her about his involvement in the Michael Smith killing forty years ago. "Because he didn't say something sooner, everything he did on this case is going to be suspect," she told them. "The three of us are going to have to walk back through his investigation. Otherwise, we're all going to be suspected of covering up for him."

"So where does Michaelson come in?" Joe wondered.

"Someone is going to the DA with information from this office. I don't know who. I know it's not either one of you. I'm certain it's not Trudy and pretty sure it's not Nick. That leaves Lennie and Jeremy in the medical examiner's office. Michaelson has been finding out things about this case before I have. That can't happen with Ernie. I have to file formal suspension papers on him before five today, but that gives us a few hours to create some doubt that it could be him."

Ed nodded. "You can trust Nick. And David, too, come to think of it. He's crazy irresponsible sometimes, but he's loyal to you, Sheriff."

"When he's not trying to take my job," Sharyn replied.

"Yeah. Even then, he wouldn't blab to Michaelson. Nobody here likes that man or has any respect for him," Ed added.

"What would Jeremy or Lennie gain from getting the DA's attention?" Joe asked.

Sharyn shrugged. "I'm not sure. Lennie has plans to be the next DA of Diamond Springs. Jeremy wants to fit in. You figure it out. I only know there's a leak. But I know I can trust you with this."

Ed and Joe glanced at each other.

"So, we'll be investigating Ernie?" Ed queried painfully.

"Not exactly. We're just going over his part of the investigation into this case to keep everything clean and equal. Any information he found has to be considered tainted."

Joe ran his hand around the back of his neck. "I hate this job sometimes."

"We can try to help Ernie," she reminded him. "Otherwise, he's going to be in jail tomorrow. We all know that. He had motive, opportunity, and access, and his alibi is worse than the judge's. He was standing here in the office when Beau was murdered.

I can't even say I know where he was the whole time. Michaelson was willing to believe the judge sneaked in here and killed Beau. Ernie was absent long enough to have knocked that statue from the roof on top of the judge as he walked by. He knew he was going to be implicated at some point. He wanted to keep Judge Hamilton quiet. He was out at the lake this morning when the judge was attacked and the fire was started."

"And he was the one who found you after the attack,' Ed continued thoughtfully. "He might not have known it was you, but when he found out, that's why he didn't kill you."

Joe glared at him. "Ernie Watkins didn't kill anyone! I don't know what happened with that kid forty years ago. At this point, we don't even know if that kid was real. But I do know Ernie didn't kill Beau Richmond or attack the sheriff and the judge!"

"I wasn't saying he did," Ed replied quietly. "I was thinking like the DA is gonna think. You better start if we're gonna help him."

Sharyn nodded. "Ed's right, Joe. Michaelson is going to put the worst possible face on this and I can't say I blame him. It'll look like we knew from the beginning and helped cover it up for Ernie. If this were anyone else, I would've arrested him right away. But we have a small window of opportunity here to look for the real killer. I have to file the suspension papers before Michaelson finds out what's going on to keep this office clear of any charges of collusion."

"It's gonna be bad enough," Ed told her. "They're gonna be looking at us under a microscope for months, even if we clear Ernie."

"Michaelson!" Joe hissed as the ADA turned the door handle.

"So, we know what we have to do," Sharyn concluded without missing a beat. "Let's get it done."

Both men nodded curtly to her then walked past Michaelson without saying a word.

"What was that all about?" he wanted to know.

"We're working on a murder case," she informed him as though he were a child. "Ed and Joe are on their way out to see how the judge is doing."

"Well, your other deputy botched the job," he delighted in telling her.

"Who is that?"

"Ernie Watkins." He put a report down on the table. "Impound says the brakes on the judge's car were definitely tampered with. If we would've known that yesterday, we could have prevented his almost tragic death."

Sharyn sighed. "It must be hard to go through life talking in sound bites."

Michaelson's face turned red. "Your deputies are dropping the ball, Sheriff. You're in charge here. I expect you to take care of the situation. This case is priority. We have a distinguished businessman and philanthropist murdered right in the middle of the sheriff's office, then an important judge has two attempts on his life and a third that might yet be fatal! You can make jokes if you like, Sheriff, but you could lose your badge for this."

She turned to him. "I'm doing my job just fine, Mr. Michaelson. We'll find out who did these things. Without you barking at my legs every five minutes!"

Michaelson almost growled at her, he was so angry. "I'd appreciate you keeping your mother's boyfriends out of this, too, Sheriff. This is a local problem. We'll take care of it locally."

"My mother's—" Sharyn thought quickly. Caison!

"The senator paid the DA a visit and asked him to take me off the case. Fortunately, Mr. Winter knows that when I'm doing a good job, people squeal the loudest."

"I didn't ask Senator Talbot to intervene," she defended hotly.

He snickered. "It must be nice to have powerful men chasing after your mother. Almost as nice as having such a personal relationship with the medical examiner's office!"

Sharyn had only once acted out in anger since she'd put on the uniform. It had happened when she'd helped catch her father's killers. She swore she wouldn't do it again. Michaelson was a petty heckler with a big agenda. She wouldn't let him goad her any further.

"You should know," she volleyed back at him.

"What does that mean?"

She stared hard at him. "I know about your little snitch, Michaelson. Did you think I wouldn't find out?"

He cracked a smile. "You're getting paranoid, Sheriff. I do my own work." He straightened his tie. "The DA expects an arrest on this case by the end of the week. Mr. Winter can be pretty formidable. I wouldn't let him down."

Sharyn watched him leave the office and saw Trudy stick her tongue out at his back as he passed her. Then she took a deep breath and slipped out the back of the office. The reporters were beginning to smell blood. A few were already looking for her. She didn't want to take a chance on giving anything away. As long as Michaelson was handing out statements about the investigation, she was going to stay clear of it.

And she was going to have to eat some crow. It was her least favorite dish, but she had all but accused Nick of giving information to the DA's office. She needed his help since she was afraid to trust Jeremy with the information. She didn't want anyone to build a career on Ernie's disgrace.

As she stood in line to buy takeout Italian food and a cheap bottle of red wine, she thought about Caison trying to come to her rescue. Usually he was giving her a hard time. Was he truly so in love with her mother that he was starting to consider her as family? She shook her head. *That* could be even worse than him working against her!

With her food as a peace offering, Sharyn drove to the college where she knew Nick would be finishing up his morning class. She slid into the back of the classroom and took a seat.

Nick was wearing heavy, dark-rimmed glasses and pacing back and forth, reading quickly from a large textbook. The large group of students were writing as hard as they could, yet most of them had tape recorders on their desks. Nick was firing off questions and statements. His passion and enthusiasm were palpable. She wondered why he was so different when he was working as the medical examiner.

Maybe it was her, she decided, watching him in fascination. She'd never heard her father say anything about him not showing up or taking naps on a murder site. T. Raymond Howard had thought the world of Nick, even though he was a "city fella." She remembered the grim look on Nick's face when he had given her the report about her father's autopsy. And she thought about the picnic he'd set for her in the mountains one long, starry night.

The class was breaking up and Sharyn shifted uncomfortably. Nick had taken off his glasses. He was staring at her as the students filed out.

"Lunch?" she asked from the back of the big room.

NINE

"It's BARELY TEN," he said coldly, picking up his textbooks and cramming them into a huge satchel. "I'm supposed to get back and help Jeremy sort through what he found in the cemetery."

"I'm sorry, Nick," she said simply.

He zipped the satchel closed and looked up at her. "Gee, does that mean I'm on the sheriff's list of trustworthy workers again?"

She looked at the bag in her hands. "I never really thought—"

"Yes, you did. You're a terrible liar, Sharyn."

"I need your help."

"What else is new?"

"Ernie confessed to being with Judge Hamilton and Beau Richmond when they killed that boy."

Nick sat down in his chair. "Ernie?"

"He belongs to Michaelson tomorrow when I file his suspension papers, Nick. We only have today."

He glanced at her and opened the bag she'd put down on his desk. "You're taking a whale of a chance with your own career," he observed, taking out the baked ziti she'd brought. He smelled it.

"I know. But we both know Ernie didn't kill Beau Richmond."

"I didn't have breakfast," he said, looking at the wine and the crisp bread. "I suppose I could eat."

Over the meal, Sharyn explained the whole dilemma to him. He took it all in while he ate, then wiped his hands on the moist towelettes that had come with the meal.

"I'll do whatever you want to help Ernie," he told her. "But I have to have your word that *this* is never going to happen again."

"Lunch?" she questioned lightly.

He grimaced. "Come on, Sharyn. I swear to you that if you ever doubt me again, question my loyalty, or think I would rat you out to that idiot Michaelson or anyone like him, I'll leave. I'm not kidding."

"All right."

He shook his head. "I want your word, Sheriff Howard. We might have our differences from time to time, but you'll never wonder again if you can trust me."

Their eyes locked and Sharyn nodded her head. "You have my word, Nick. I'll never doubt you again."

He looked away and picked up the napkin again. "Good. Let's go help Ernie."

They drove out to Judge Hamilton's house. The fire had engulfed it, leaving nothing but charred remains and soaking debris. They walked through the house and garage. The fire chief was there and offered his finds on the fire.

"It was started here in the garage when someone threw gasoline from the car on the walls. There was gasoline on the car, too, but a lot of it had evaporated. Otherwise you probably wouldn't have been able to make that dramatic rescue, Sheriff."

"Was that the only set place?" she wondered, not wanting to get into her daring rescue again. The chief had already protested to the commissioners that she had gone into the house inappropriately.

"No," he admitted and walked them to another part of the house. "We found evidence of chemical starter here. Lighter fluid, maybe. Like they use on grills. I think it might have been the judge's study."

"There's not enough here to guess at," Nick told her, sifting through some of what was on the ground. "If the answer is here, we won't find it."

"Thanks, Chief," Sharyn said to the husky, red-faced man. She shook his hand. "I wouldn't undercut your job if a man's life hadn't been at stake."

He looked down at the soot on his boots. "I guess I know that, Sheriff. It's just that there are rules."

Nick stared at him. "Let's hope she doesn't remember that if it comes to *your* life, huh, Chief?"

They walked out of the debris and got back in Sharyn's Jeep. "I still have the search warrant for the judge's office," she told him. "Let's hope we can find something there."

"What are we looking for?" he wondered.

"I don't know," she revealed. "Something that the killer might have forgotten. Something that will create doubt that Ernie could be the killer."

"Like a written confession?" he asked.

She gave him a withering glance. "You just see what you can find in the office as far as unusual prints. I'll look for anything else."

"When will you have to file the suspension papers?"

"Before five today," she told him. "I sent Ernie home after the fire but I won't officially suspend him until then. That's my prerogative as sheriff, in case someone asks."

"Which you know they will," he added.

"I have time to investigate his actions before making it official. They can give me a hard time about the case and how it looks, but I'm following the rules."

"For once?"

"I'm not a rule breaker," she said. "I do what has to be done but usually I stay within the guidelines. I wouldn't let someone die for the regs, though. I know the chief has a good response time and he doesn't want to look bad either. It was an unusual situation."

"Whatever you say," he answered blandly.

"It was. I'm not."

"Okay."

She shook her head. "You're as infuriating as Michaelson!"

"Because I'm truthful?"

"Never mind."

They parked in the garage where the judge always parked his car. It seemed an odd imposition to be in his place.

"How's he doing?" Nick wondered as they started down to the courthouse.

"He's still alive. That's about all the doctor will say. He isn't optimistic. The head injury was bad enough without him being in the trunk of the car with the garage on fire."

"Sounds like one of your days," he told her.

Sharyn stopped walking. "Giving you my word that I trust you didn't set the stage for you to criticize everything I do."

He didn't stop. "That was a right I had before. Are you coming or what?

She gritted her teeth then followed him to the elevator. "I should have told you I would never trust you again and hope that you left!" she muttered.

The judge's personal assistant was reluctant to show them into his office. "This hardly seems the time or place to show such disrespect for him. He's lying in a hospital room, possibly dying, and you're going through his papers, trying to prove he murdered one of his friends."

Sharyn took a deep breath. "I'm not trying to prove the judge murdered anyone. Unless he purposely attacked himself and made it look like someone else did it, he's not guilty of Mr. Richmond's murder. I'm trying to find out who did this to him."

The woman sniffed and wiped at her eyes. "Still, it hardly seems right."

"I have a warrant," Sharyn told her grimly. She put it on the woman's desk. "We'll try not to disturb anything."

They walked in through the double doors in the judge's private chamber. Nick closed the doors on the assistant's unhappy face.

"Wow! What a place!"

"You haven't been up here?" Sharyn asked.

He shrugged. "They keep me in the hospital basement with the stiffs and don't let me out much."

Sharyn ignored him and let him do his job while she did hers. The judge had a wealth of private papers. Documents were carefully kept and diligently filed. The man was rigorous in specifying dates and people.

"You know," Nick remarked as he went over the office, "one thing struck me about Beau's death. Everything was clean around Beau. Even though the table hadn't been wiped clean. *Your* fingerprints were all over everything. But his clothes and the belt were stripped. And none of his fingerprints were on the table, even though he'd been in the room with David."

"What does that mean?" she asked, sifting through a file.

"I don't know," he admitted. "It's just unusual. Like the killer was trying to strip Beau of his identity as much as he could."

Sharyn paused. "How could that have happened so quickly? He barely had time to attack Beau and hang him."

"He wouldn't have had any time if Matthews hadn't left the room," Nick commented. "If you were going to suspend anyone, it should be him."

"David couldn't know he was being stalked and Beau wasn't officially in custody. He was baby-sitting him without knowing why."

"He was careless and sloppy and you're making excuses for him," Nick read into her statement. "Why do you feel so guilty about that guy?"

"I don't feel guilty about him," she responded defensively. "I just think the situation was extreme and I don't think David is to blame for that. You've done the same thing with Jeremy."

"Jeremy tries. That's more than I can say for Matthews." He crouched down beside a chair at the front of the desk. "Have you thought about Lennie being the killer?"

"What?"

"Lennie," he repeated. "He had the same opportunity that Ernie had. We don't know that much about him, besides him being a football player and a smart mouth who likes to follow you around."

"We work together," she protested. "He isn't following me around."

"Have you questioned him about where he was during those times?"

"There's no connection," she answered. "Why would he kill Beau or attack the judge?"

"What's the connection between the judge and Beau? A murder that may or may not have happened forty years ago? If that's the case, why hasn't Ernie been attacked? He confessed to being there. And what's your theory? A crazed relative is going around exacting justice for Michael Smith's death at the school?"

"I have Lennie checking into that angle," she admitted.

"Sharyn, there's no proof this boy did anything except wander away and not go back to the school like a hundred other boys. Beau was crazy and dug up some other boy's bones, thinking that they belonged to Michael Smith."

"How do you explain the attack on the judge?"

"The two might not even be part of the same thing," he theorized. "Or Lennie did them both."

Sharyn sat back in the judge's big chair and laughed. "You're crazy!"

He glanced up at her. "Lennie *is* from Diamond Springs. He came back just in time for these things to happen and he's ambitious. Maybe he's going to solve the case and take the credit for it."

She opened up another of the judge's files as she shook her head. "What do you have against poor Lennie?"

"Poor Lennie?" he questioned. "He's six foot two, wears a Superbowl ring, and drives a Jaguar. What's poor about him?"

She didn't respond and he looked at her again.

"Sharyn? Did you find something?"

"Nick, the judge was being blackmailed."

"What?" He walked behind the desk where she was sitting and looked over her shoulder at the file spread out on the desk.

"Look at this stuff." She spread out letters written by a childish hand in crayon. There were drawings of a small figure in a grave and threats to expose the judge for his part in Michael Smith's death. And there were canceled checks. "He's been paying off on this for the past ten years. Look at the dates!"

"Try not to touch any more of it. There could be prints here that we can trace to the blackmailer."

Sharyn looked at him. "So the judge was *really* haunted by what happened that night at the boys' school. The blackmailer probably found out who he was and wanted his fair share."

"But not Beau?" Nick wondered. "Beau was worth a lot more money."

She shrugged. "We looked through all of Beau's things but we didn't find a blackmail file."

"Maybe he just snapped?"

"Maybe."

There was another picture of the same group of boys at Jefferson. It was the same picture taken by the bridge. The same face was circled.

"Someone else knew about what happened to Michael Smith," she said thoughtfully. "Maybe Beau wouldn't pay. Maybe that was the problem. Maybe the judge was threatening to stop paying, too."

"I'm taking this back to the lab," he said quietly. "It's four forty-five. I'll send you a copy of one of the checks so you can get in touch with the bank."

"All right," she agreed. "Thanks for your help, Nick."

"Will this be enough to get Ernie off?"

She shook her head. "Think about it. If anything, it might be motive for his actions. He's another person who knew about Michael Smith being killed. And neither man told us about him being there. It makes him look even worse."

"Great," he said morosely. "Glad I could be such a big help."

She put her hand on his shoulder, then jumped back when he turned to face her. "He'll be fine," she hastened to assure him. "I'm sure he's innocent. We just have to prove it."

Filing Ernie's suspension papers was the hardest job Sharyn had ever done with the department. She gave them to Trudy at 4:55.

Trudy looked at them and gasped. "Sheriff!"

Sharyn shook her head. "Do it, Trudy. I've done what I could for him."

Ed and Joe returned after a grueling day of re-examining Ernie's parts of the investigations. Everything was fine, as far as their reports could tell. Sharyn wasn't sure if they would tell her if something was wrong. She knew if *she* thought about that, then Michaelson was going to think it as well.

Lennie came in to tell her that he couldn't find any members of Michael Smith's family living in the area. He was still looking up old records, but so far the search had turned out to be less than productive.

Sharyn took a deep breath then told him about Ernie's suspension. She explained the situation to him, urging him silently not to be the one to take it to Michaelson.

At 5:00 sharp, there was a call from Michaelson.

"Why haven't you picked up Ernie Watkins, Sheriff?" he demanded.

"He's suspended without pay until the investigation is over," she stated flatly.

"That wasn't the question. With Hamilton in the hospital, Deputy Watkins looks like the prime suspect to me. Can you give me any reason why you wouldn't arrest him?"

Sharyn wished she could smash the phone on the desktop. "No, I can't."

"Then I suggest you do so, Sheriff. I'll be ready to arraign him tomorrow."

"I have some new evidence that your contact doesn't know about," Sharyn told him quickly. "Judge Hamilton was being blackmailed for the killing of Michael Smith at Jefferson."

"So, we're filing on blackmail charges for the deputy as well?"

"We don't know who blackmailed the judge yet."

"So you can't prove Deputy Watkins *wasn't* blackmailing him?"

"Michaelson—"

"Pick him up, Sheriff. Or I'll have someone else do it for you."

The phone went dead in her hand. There was a knock on the door and she looked up to see Ernie's face come around the corner like always.

"It struck me that the safest place for me right

now might be in jail," Ernie told her quietly. "I'm here to turn myself in."

Ed and Joe flatly refused to put handcuffs on Ernie. Annie waited at the station with Ernie, holding his hand and sitting miserably beside him in the conference room. Michaelson came in with a bevy of reporters about an hour later. He announced, boldly, that the case had been solved and that the accused killer was off the streets. David came in and Sharyn had the bewildered deputy take Ernie down to a holding cell.

She tried not to look at Ernie as David was taking him down. The only thing she could do to help him now was to find the real killer. Hanging around the office, feeling bad about the whole thing, was only going to land him in arraignment the next day. She couldn't stop the process but she could find the right person to go through it.

The reporters Michaelson let into the office turned to her as Ernie was taken away. Sharyn told them firmly that they were still investigating the case and that even thought Ernie had been arrested she was standing by her deputy. Ernie Watkins wasn't the killer. Then she dismissed them from the station. Ed and Joe gladly showed the reporters the front door.

Five minutes later, there was a call directly from the DA's office. Jack Winter wanted to see her. Right away.

Sharyn put on her hat and walked down to the DA's office in the courthouse. It was dark already. The stars were bright above the black mounds of the Uwharries that edged the horizon. The lake was shiny black, reflecting the lights of the town. A new crescent of the moon was barely rising above the old mountains. Her breath was frosty in the evening air.

She knew the DA was staying late for her. That was never a good sign. She had only met Jack Winter briefly but she'd seen him in court many times. He was formidable. She'd also heard he was a bad man to have for an enemy. So far, they hadn't crossed paths, even in the worst of times.

Investigating misconduct in her own department made this a unique time, she supposed. She wished she had Ernie standing at her side. At that moment she wished she hadn't ever put on the badge and strapped her grandfather's gun to her hip. She could be home, watching television and eating nachos and not realizing that a good man's life was at stake. It wouldn't surprise her for Michaelson to ask for the death penalty on this one.

Diamond Springs had changed radically from the time when she was a child. Not that people were afraid to walk down the tree-lined streets or go to sleep in their beds. It was a subtle difference in character as the old times and attitudes shifted and the new people and ideas came in to take their place.

She knew her father would've hated it. He didn't like change and he liked his town the way it was.

She wasn't sure she liked it. Jack Winter's assistant greeted her in hushed tones. She liked the way it had been when she was a child, too. Things were changing, though. There was no stopping them. She couldn't go back and make things different. For her, or for Ernie. All she could do was to help shape the future and try to hold on to the present.

The DA's assistant showed Sharyn into the big, plush office. It was as large as Judge Hamilton's office but without the regal ambiance of the judge's chamber. Instead, Jack Winter was a man of impeccable taste. From the paintings on the wall to the rich carpet underfoot, Sharyn knew this was a man who valued refinement.

"Drink, Sheriff?" the DA asked from the back corner of the room.

Sharyn jumped a little in surprise. She realized immediately that it was a strategic maneuver. Winter could observe those coming into his office before they realized that he was standing there behind them. Very clever.

"No, thanks, I'm still on duty," she replied briskly. She held her hat in her hands and her head high. If she were going to get reprimanded, she wasn't going to take it passively.

"Of course," he acknowledged. "I wasn't suggesting something alcoholic, Sheriff. Coffee, perhaps? Hot chocolate?"

"No, thanks," she answered quietly. "Let's get this over with."

He gestured that she should take a seat and he sat behind the imposing black desk. "I was looking forward to a visit with you, Sheriff. We rarely cross each other's paths."

Sharyn took a seat and realized that the chairs were lower to the floor. Again a strategy to put Winter's visitors on a lower level. She sat on the edge of the seat and looked at him across the black lacquer finish of his desk.

"Sir, I'm in the middle of an investigation and I know you didn't call me in here for chitchat. So, if we could dispense with the banter and get right to the point, I'd appreciate it."

For a long moment, she thought the formidable Jack Winter was going to get angry. Ernie had told her when she was first elected sheriff that he was a man she needed to steer clear of. Her father had avoided him. T. Raymond had said that when Jack Winter shook your hand, you'd better count your fingers. He had been DA for a very long time and knew where most of the secrets were buried in the county. And who to squeeze for them.

Then he smiled at her. There was something about him that was extremely attractive and yet repellent.

He was slick, she considered, and clever. It was more than that. You had the feeling that he knew things about you. Things that you hadn't shared with anyone else. He made her feel as if she was sitting there with him dressed in her old pajamas.

"You are everything I've heard about you, Sheriff," he complimented her in the rich voice that had won a thousand court battles for the county. "A little precipitous but you'll learn."

"Mr. Winter—" she began.

"Jack," he corrected, sitting forward in his chair. "And I'll call you Sharyn. I'm sure we're going to be great friends."

Since they barely knew each other, she doubted that but she kept her peace.

"Sharyn, do you know who your enemies are?" he wondered, studying her face.

She shook her head. "I don't think I actually have enemies, unless you count criminals I've put in prison."

"Think again."

She looked back at him, wondering where this strange conversation was leading. "All right."

"Michaelson is our common enemy, Sharyn," he related to her briefly.

Sharyn looked into his pale blue eyes. Winter wasn't a handsome man but he was a compelling one. She found herself unable to look away. "Why?"

"Why am I telling you this?" he asked. "I'll assume you understand the underlying threat to yourself. Michaelson wants my job. I don't intend to relinquish it. There is nowhere for him to go from here. It would be best for both of us if he were replaced."

"Replaced?" She shook her head and formulated more complex speech. "If you want to replace Michaelson, why don't you just replace him? You're his boss."

"Not exactly. I have to give him time to alienate anyone who might be his ally."

"I know you don't think *I'm* his ally."

"I wasn't sure until I saw you on television. You made your contempt for him very clear."

Sharyn shook her head. "All I said was that I stood behind Deputy Watkins and I was still investigating."

He smiled. "That, just after ADA Michaelson told everyone that he had made an arrest and it was safe to walk the streets again. I think you see my point."

"What is it you want from me, Mr. Winter?"

"Jack," he coaxed.

"Jack." She complied for the sake of expediency.

He looked triumphant. "I want to you to continue to investigate, Sheriff, and clear Deputy Watkins. That's all you need do. I'll take care of the rest."

Sharyn nodded. "That's my plan, Mr.—Jack."

"Fine. Good luck, then, Sheriff. I have my eye on you. And I'll be in touch."

Sharyn felt dismissed yet at the same time, threatened. The idea of him watching her was disturbing. "I'll let you know what I find," she promised.

"No need," he excused her. "I have my sources."

"Lennie Albert?" she asked him. "Is he one of your sources?"

Jack Winter smiled warmly but his eyes were cold enough to cut to the bone. "If I told you all my secrets, Sheriff, I'd have to replace *you,* wouldn't I?"

Sharyn didn't say anything more. His smooth voice and cold eyes were enough to freeze her blood. She nodded to him and left his office.

Jeremy was waiting in the street for her. He was moving his hands around and stamping his feet. The wind had picked up off the lake and the night was freezing with it.

Sharyn, still unraveled by her talk with Jack Winter, was surprised. Since she knew it was Lennie, not Jeremy, feeding the DA information, she was pleased to see him.

"I have to see you, Sheriff," he told her.

"It must be important to wait out here in the cold for me."

"Trudy told me where you were," he explained. "It's about the cemetery and the bones. I think I might know something about Michael Smith."

"All right," she agreed, wishing she could go home and call it a day. "Do you want to go back to the office?"

"Oh, no," he said quickly. "You'll have to come back to the lab with me. I'll have to show you."

"Can this wait until tomorrow?"

"This is very important," he told her plainly. "It could save Deputy Watkins's career."

She sighed. "Okay. Let me get my Jeep."

"I have my car right over here," he said to her. "We could just go in that."

Sharyn glanced at the office, considering whether or not she should tell someone that she was going. She wasn't wearing her radio and had left her gun hanging in her office. But she was only going to the hospital lab. Surely whatever he had to show her wouldn't take that long.

"All right." She followed him to his car and climbed in the front seat beside him. The car shell immediately cut the wind and she felt warmer.

Jeremy started the car and pulled out into the busy street. "You know, Sheriff, I like you," he said in a light voice. "You're good at what you do but you don't step on anybody to get the job done."

"Thanks, Jeremy," she answered. "I hope things work out for you here."

He smiled at her quickly. "Things have a way of working out, don't they, Sheriff? Especially justice.

No matter what we do or who we become, justice follows us for the things that we do. The Greeks called it just retribution. They even sent the Furies after people who did terrible things to other people. That would make your job easier, wouldn't it?"

Sharyn laughed. "A band of ugly, mean women with sharp claws going around ripping apart the bad guys? Yeah. That probably would make it easy."

Jeremy pulled the car into his space by the hospital basement. They walked in together, Jeremy switching on the lights as he went. "Nick was done working for the night. He went home," Jeremy explained to her. "He works hard at what he does."

"Yes, he does," she agreed. "What did you find, Jeremy?"

"You'll have to see it," he said briefly. "In here." He led her into the lab but the light wouldn't turn on when he flicked the switch. He did it a few more times but the light still wouldn't come on. "Wait here, please. The fuse box gets cranky down here sometimes. I'll be right back."

Sharyn waited for a moment then saw a small light on in the cubbyhole that was Jeremy's office at the back of the lab. She walked back to it and sat at his desk. There were reports and case files covering the surface. She glanced through them. She'd seen all of them on her own desk. None of them were enough to prove Ernie's innocence.

Her eye caught a copy of the picture of the boys at Jefferson, standing by the bridge that they were building. It was the same picture but none of the boys' faces had been circled. She knew Jeremy had been going through the old training school files for Nick.

She remembered him talking about the old school at the chapel that night when they found the boy's remains and how upset Ernie had become. She'd thought it was just Ernie being strange but now she knew it was more.

Sharyn started to turn the picture over and caught a glimpse of handwriting on the back. Then the lights went completely out around her.

"Jeremy?" she called out. "Do you need some help?"

There was no response. She got up from the desk and walked into the main part of the lab. It was totally black in the basement with no light from outside sources to guide her. She walked into a table and put her hand out to try to find her way.

"Jeremy?"

She heard something and reached for her gun, remembering too late that she had left it in the office. Instinctively, she dropped to the cold concrete floor. The lights flashed on around her and she blinked her eyes.

"Sharyn?"

It was Nick. She got up and brushed off her hands. "In here."

He opened the lab door and stared at her curiously. "What are you doing in here?"

"I'm here with Jeremy. He said he had something he wanted to show me about Michael Smith."

Nick glanced around. "Why were all of the lights out?"

"I don't know. Jeremy said you'd gone home for the night."

"I never turn off all the lights."

"Where is he?" she wondered, walking past him and into the hall. "Jeremy?"

The man walked out of a storage closet, adjusting his glasses with a sheepish expression on his face. "I guess I got lost trying to find the fuse box. Sorry."

"What did you want to show me about Michael Smith?" she asked, starting to get impatient.

Jeremy glanced at Nick hesitantly. "It can wait."

Sharyn gritted her teeth. "I thought it was urgent."

"I made a mistake, a miscalculation. I just realized it."

Sharyn shook her head. "Well, let me know when you recalculate."

"I will," he promised. "I hope it's not too late."

Nick drew in an impatient breath. "I have some news for you, if you're done here."

She smiled at Jeremy, who smiled back at her. "I guess I am for right now. What is it?"

"We have to go to Atlanta."

"What?"

"Tonight."

TEN

SHARYN WAS IN Nick's black Cadillac and they were
on their way to Atlanta before she had much time
to think about it. He had a police radio in his car.
She called in to the office to let them know what
was going on.

"We'll hold the fort, Sheriff," David told her con-
fidently. "Pretty quiet tonight anyway."

"How's Ernie holding up?" she wondered.

"He's quiet. Not like himself, but who would be?"

Sharyn told him that she would call back later.
Then she looked at Nick's profile in the passing
streetlights. "Tell me again why we have to go to
Atlanta tonight?"

He switched on the interior light. "Take a look at
those checks."

She obliged him, looking at the copies he'd made
from the originals. "They're all deposited into the
same bank in Atlanta. Any prints?"

"No, they're clean. But the checks have been deposited into the same account for the last ten years.
A business account. I typed the number into the

automated phone system for the bank. It wouldn't let me access the account but it did tell me that it was a business account."

"All right."

He glanced at her. "I have a friend on the job in Atlanta, Frank Hardin. He's going to help us get access to those bank records. To *Lennie's* bank records."

"You found Lennie's name on something?" she questioned quickly.

"No, but I think you can stop looking for anyone else."

"Why?"

"First of all, Lennie is from Atlanta."

"So are a lot of other people."

"Second, Lennie played football for the Falcons but he was up to his rear in debts. Hardin told me that the last injury Lennie had wasn't from playing football. The police tried to get him to name names but he wouldn't. Then he quit the Falcons, citing injuries, and moved back home to Diamond Springs."

"But that was only a year ago. These checks date back a lot longer," she reminded him.

"Lennie found out about what happened at the school. He knows a lot about its history. Maybe he did research that pointed to what happened to Michael Smith and he started blackmailing the judge. But when he got back home, he wanted more. So he started blackmailing or trying to blackmail Beau Richmond. But Beau wasn't stable enough to take the pressure and he cracked. Lennie had to get rid of him before he had a chance to tell anyone."

Sharyn considered all of it silently. It didn't make any sense to her but she could see where the possibilities fit together. "This is a weaker case than the one against Ernie."

"It won't be when we get the bank records," he told her triumphantly.

"Are you trying to get my job?" she wondered.

"Sheriff Thomopolis," he tried it out. "I suppose it does have a certain ring to it."

She told him about the conversation she'd had with Jack Winter. "He's a strange man."

"And a dangerous one," Nick added. "His enemies, as he put it, have a habit of disappearing."

"So, he's like the Godfather DA?"

Nick shrugged. "Talk to anyone. Winter is a man people don't mess around with."

"Ernie told me that when I became Sheriff," she said softly, thinking about Ernie being in jail.

"You and Ernie are close," he observed. "It must have been a shock to you when he and Annie got back together."

"We're not close like that," she informed him. "He was around when I was a kid. In a way, he reminds me a lot of my father. Sometimes when I hear Ernie talking, something he says sounds just like something my dad would say."

"So, you think of Ernie like a *father?*" Nick asked with something like amazement in his tone.

She shook her head in disbelief. "Did you think we were *romantically* involved?"

"I didn't know," he admitted. "You spent a lot of time together, and then when he took up with Annie, you seemed to be interested in Lennie."

"What?"

"You spend a lot of time together."

She took in a deep breath and asked heaven for patience. "We work together."

"I know."

Sharyn shrugged and folded her arms across her chest. "Not that I have time to be romantically involved with anyone."

"It would be easier if it was someone you worked with," he remarked.

"I suppose that's true," she admitted. "I spend a lot of time at work."

"But if you think of Ernie like a father," Nick speculated, "you must think of Ed and Joe that way, too."

"Not exactly, but Joe is married and Ed is, well, Ed."

"Women like Ed," Nick said.

"I like Ed, too. Just not that way."

"Well, that leaves David, who is close to your own age," Nick continued.

"He and I graduated the same year," she agreed.

"Are you…attracted to David?"

"Nick!"

He put a hand through his hair. "I'm going to pull over and get some gas and something to drink. You want something?"

"I'll get out, too."

They stopped at a gas station just across the Georgia state line. Sharyn picked up a drink and a sandwich because she hadn't had dinner. Nick glanced at the sandwich in her hand as she got back in the car.

"Don't even tell me I can't eat in your car," she told him brutally. "You dragged me down here for this. I'm hungry."

He grimaced. "Things get spilled in cars."

"I'm not going to spill a sandwich," she answered, opening the wrapping.

Nick looked away as he started the car. "Just don't forget to take out the wrapper at the next stop."

"You sound like my mother," she accused around a mouthful of food.

"Great," he muttered.

"What?"

"Nothing."

Halfway to Atlanta, Sharyn offered to drive.

They could switch off and neither of them would be so tired.

"That's okay," he said with a quick, defensive smile.

She rolled her eyes. "You don't let anyone else drive your car?"

"I'm fine," he answered. "You've had a few hard days. Try to get some rest."

"I'm fine," she replied. But she sat on her side of the car, thinking about everything that had happened.

Could Lennie be responsible? It sounded outlandish but she knew in her heart that Ernie hadn't killed Beau Richmond. Judge Hamilton had been the victim rather than the predator. There was no one else who could have known about Michael Smith's death.

"You know, there's something that's bothering me in all of this," she spoke out loud.

"Besides the obvious."

"We know that Beau was responsible for putting the boy's bones in the chapel. We've assumed that the killer followed me to the cemetery that night and hit me in the head so he could take something that was left behind because he knew Beau had dug up the remains. We've assumed whatever was there incriminated the killer."

"Okay," he agreed. "And?"

"First of all, if you were the killer, wouldn't you

have killed Beau in the cemetery, if you had the chance? It would've been a better opportunity than the sheriff's department."

"Unless the killer didn't need to kill Beau until he started to spill the story," Nick suggested.

"Okay. But second, if Beau thought that the grave was Michael Smith's, why didn't the killer think so? He didn't attack Beau at the cemetery, so the chances are that Beau never knew he was there. The only reason the killer would have to go back to the cemetery is because he knew that body wasn't Michael Smith's. He took whatever was on the boy's arm that was in the grave, so that we wouldn't know who the boy was."

"I suppose that makes sense," he agreed.

"How far yet?" she asked as they began to get close to Atlanta.

Nick caught the urgency in her tone. "Just a few minutes."

FRANK HARDIN had been a detective for twelve years. His jacket was wrinkled and the shirt he wore had a food stain on the collar but he had a sharp eye and he was happy to see Nick.

"This guy is like family," he told Sharyn. "Anytime you decide to turn him loose, Sheriff, we'll take him."

"Thanks, Frank," Nick said with a trace of embarrassment. "Did you get those records?"

"As a matter of fact, the vice president of the bank told me that he had to stay here with the files until he could take them back. I gave him a choice: wait for you to get here or leave them and I'd get them back to him tomorrow. He went home and went to sleep." He put the files on the desk. "Help yourself."

Nick sat beside Sharyn as they opened up the bank records. The account was opened ten years before in the company name of Palladin, Inc. The man who cashed the checks was the head of the company. Michael Smith.

"Is that some weird sense of humor?" Nick asked blankly.

"No," Sharyn replied, her brain working overtime. "No, it's not weird at all. Michael Smith isn't dead."

"The boy they all remember killing? The murder the judge was being blackmailed for?"

"The body we didn't find," she added. "Don't you see? He didn't die. He was exactly what you've been saying all along, one of the runaways. But they thought he was dead. At least Ernie and Beau did. That's why the judge was so sure the boy was alive. Because Michael Smith was blackmailing him. They shared the terrible secret all these years."

"So why kill the golden goose?" Nick wondered.

"Maybe Michael wanted more. He came back to Diamond Springs and realized how wealthy Beau was. What he didn't realize was that Beau was having emotional problems, and when he heard from Michael Smith, it drove him over the edge. Michael didn't want to kill him. He wanted his money. Then the whole thing came out and he panicked, so he had to get rid of the judge, too."

"So it couldn't be Lennie," Nick accepted gracefully.

Sharyn shook her head. "No, not Lennie. Lennie's caught up in this thing with Winter and Michaelson. He sold me out for his own gain so the DA could destroy Michaelson and he could take his place."

"But who else?"

"Jeremy," she said slowly. "Jeremy is really Michael Smith."

"What?"

"Think about it. He had a lot of knowledge about the school. He ruffled Ernie's feathers with it that first night. The mistakes he made on the autopsy and the attempt on the judge's life weren't mistakes. He did it on purpose to keep us off track. He came back to the cemetery that night to get the jewelry that had been left behind because he knew I was going to find it. Only the person who put the unknown boy there would know what to look for. Jeremy knew it was missing when the bones came back from Raleigh. Until then, he probably thought it was intact and he could just grab it before anyone noticed."

"But we checked his prints and his ID before

we hired him. The county always does that," Nick argued. "Jeremy Lambert was clean. I saw his record myself."

"He's from Atlanta, right? Have your friend check him out again from this end," she suggested. "I'm going to call the office at home and have them send us Michael Smith's fingerprints."

Nick came back a short time later with Jeremy's records. "He's clean. Mother: Arnelle. Father: Victor. He graduated from the University of Atlanta. He's who he says he is for a long way back."

"How far?" Sharyn wondered.

"Huh?"

"How far back?"

"Twenty years. Back to college."

"And the bones are about twenty years old?"

Nick shrugged. "They said there was a high rate of deterioration."

Sharyn looked at Frank Hardin, who'd joined them at the desk. "Frank, could you check your missing-child folders? Say twenty years back?"

"Sure. What am I looking for?"

"A missing child named Jeremy Lambert."

"Your fax is coming through, Sheriff," another detective told her.

"Thanks," Sharyn said and went to get it from the machine.

She looked at Jeremy's fingerprints and Michael

Smith's. Even though the child's were older and grainier, there was no mistaking the print.

Nick looked at her. "Jeremy is Michael Smith."

Sharyn looked at the clock. It was just after midnight. "We have to get back."

"Ernie?"

She nodded. "He's arraigned first thing this morning. He'll probably make bail. It could be just what Michael is waiting for. He didn't ask Ernie for money and I think Jeremy might have been prepared to take me out of the picture last night at the lab when you showed up. If he can't do anything else, he might decide to get rid of Ernie."

"Do you think Ernie knows that Jeremy is Michael Smith?" Nick wondered.

"No," she denied. "Ernie's convinced he killed Michael Smith or at least helped the older boys kill him. He wouldn't suspect this."

Frank was apologetic but there was no way he could find a file for Jeremy Lambert that quickly in the middle of the night. "Those files over ten years old are here but they aren't on the computer yet. We keep missing-kid files a long time but the old ones are paper files and I'll have to sort through them."

"Thanks, Frank," Sharyn said, shaking his hand. "I appreciate your help."

"I'll let you know if we find it," he told her, taking Nick's hand and pushing his eyebrows up and down suggestively behind Sharyn's retreating back. "Not bad."

Nick grinned and shook his hand quickly. "Thanks, Frank. Talk to you later."

The drive back to Diamond Springs seemed to take an eternity. Sharyn called ahead to have David call in backup and arrest Jeremy. The deputies went out but there was no sign of Jeremy at his apartment. They put out an APB on him and his green Ford.

"At least Ernie is in a good place," she said when she heard the news. Jeremy was able to get to Beau during the crisis and the snow but he was in the conference room. Ernie was locked behind bars and the other deputies were watching out for him. Jeremy wouldn't sneak past them this time.

"You mean Annie's?" David asked her with a smile in his voice.

"What?"

"The ADA decided to arraign Ernie in night court about midnight. Annie got his bail and he went home with her. They were going to stay with her parents so Ernie'd have a whole bunch of people around him."

"Call him, David," she instructed. "Or send someone out there if you can't get through. Have him get back in there for protective custody right away."

"Sheriff?"

"Just do it," she replied harshly. "His life is in danger!"

"You know Jeremy might not want to kill Ernie," Nick hypothesized. "There hasn't been any threat against him and no money demand. Just like the judge and Beau Richmond didn't blame Ernie, maybe Michael Smith didn't blame him either."

"I hope you're right." She seethed helplessly. "I'm going to personally shake Michaelson out of his tree when we get back. What was the idea? Do this while I'm out of town? In the middle of the night? What was he thinking?"

"Obviously Winter is letting him hang himself," Nick remarked.

"I should've known when I saw that picture on Jeremy's desk," she said flatly. "It's the same picture Beau and Walter had of the school with all the boys near the half-finished bridge. His didn't have the face circled but it did have that writing on the back. I only saw it for a second before the lights went out but I think it was close to what we found on the notes the judge received."

"He had access to every clue we found. You can't blame yourself for not knowing the boy wasn't dead."

"If he hurts Ernie—"

Nick put his hand over hers on the seat between them. "I know your father was killed, Sharyn, but it doesn't mean Ernie will go that way. Everyone knows to look for Jeremy now. He can't get too far. David will take Ernie back to the office and he'll be fine."

An hour later, Ernie and Annie were still missing.

"I thought they went to her parents' house?" Sharyn demanded from David on the radio.

"Her parents said Ernie used the phone. He got upset and left. Annie insisted on going with him. That was a couple of hours ago. They don't know where they went."

"Put out an APB on Ernie's truck," she instructed. "What about Jeremy?"

"Nothing yet, Sheriff," David told her. "Joe and Ed came in. We even brought in some civilian deputies. We've been looking for Nick. Did you see him before you left?"

Sharyn glanced at Nick. "He's here with me. We went to Georgia together."

"Oh?"

Sharyn shook her head. "Never mind that. Find Ernie."

It was still dark when they arrived in Diamond Springs at 5:00 a.m. Nick had flown down the Interstate with the help of the Georgia police escorting them through that state. A heavy frost covered everything. The night had been bitterly cold.

Morning was only a short time away but Ernie and Jeremy and Annie were still missing. Even with patrols crisscrossing the county, they couldn't find them.

Sharyn knew Jeremy would've had enough time to do whatever he wanted to Ernie and Annie and not be found in the state again. There were roadblocks on all the major roads. No one was going in or out of the county without being stopped but it was a big county, full of mountains and back roads. Most of it was rural. It would be impossible to cover it all for days, even with the extended manpower.

Sharyn had Nick stop the car at Ernie's house. It was dark and Ernie's pickup was gone but Sharyn knew that Ernie kept a spare key in the garage. She opened the door and went inside.

Ernie's house was as tidy as his desk and car always were. There was no sign of a struggle.

Sharyn walked past the answering machine and glanced at it. The red light was blinking. She thought about the call Ernie had made before he left with Annie, then pushed the button and heard Jeremy's impassive voice play back for her.

"I don't know if you're home yet, Deputy Watkins, but I need you to come to A Building at the Jefferson campus. I think I found something important."

"Let's go!" she yelled for Nick, who was in the other room.

"Where?" he demanded.

"Jefferson Training School. He has them there."

Sharyn radioed Ed, David, and Joe that they were on their way to the school. Sharyn and Nick were only a few minutes from the little town where the campus nestled. She realized, halfway there, that she wasn't armed.

"My gun," she lamented.

"Take the one from the glove compartment," Nick advised. "I have a couple more in the trunk."

She glanced at him as she took out the small .32-caliber pistol. "That's a lot of guns for one person."

"I try to be prepared."

"We'll talk about this later," she advised him.

"I'm a deputy," he responded. "I'm supposed to be armed for emergencies."

"But you're not an army."

"I guess it was a good thing today," he answered smugly. "This way, I could share with you."

They approached the school campus from the south end where the trees were heaviest and it would be difficult to see the car. Nick took his pistol from the trunk and stood by the car.

"I'm going in," Sharyn said when backup didn't come just after they arrived.

"No reg-breaking there," Nick commented. "I thought the first rule was wait for backup."

"When you're a deputy," she told him. "Not when you're the sheriff. Besides, you're my backup."

"How do you want to do this so we don't shoot each other?" he wondered, feeling the cold steel in his hand.

"Each building has two entrances. I'll go in the far side; you go in this side. We'll take it one floor at a time. Don't shoot anything."

"What if he shoots at me?"

"We don't know if he's armed. He hasn't been so far," she reminded him. "Just be careful."

They split up just outside the old building. The wind was ghostly, combing through the sleeping trees with icy fingers, whistling down the empty corridors of the big old house. Around them, the other houses watched with empty gazes. It was as close to real life as some of them had come in ten years.

Sharyn felt the loose mortar in the stairs under her feet. The A house was condemned. Large signs warned that it was unsafe. She'd only gone ten feet when she walked into Annie's unconscious form on the freezing concrete. Sharyn checked her pulse. The other woman was alive but apparently injured. Probably a knock on the head, she considered. She called for an ambulance on her radio and covered Annie with her jacket. If Ernie was still alive, it was doubtful he would remain that way for long. She left Annie for the ambulance and continued up the first-floor stairs.

She could hear voices. At least they sounded like voices. With all the squeaks and groans the old house was making in the wind, she wasn't sure. She paused and caught sight of Nick's shadowy form as he ascended the next set of stairs and followed up on the opposite side.

On the second floor, she was certain of the voices. She knew Nick must hear them, too. It was two people talking, possibly Ernie and Jeremy, although she couldn't be sure. They weren't shouting, just talking. It sounded as though the sound was coming from the third floor. Sharyn managed to signal Nick at that moment. He nodded and they both went up to the third floor.

"I don't understand." She could hear Ernie's voice. He sounded deathly tired and cold.

"Why? You of all people! You know what it was like here! You know what I went through because you went through it, too. Didn't they deserve just retribution? Didn't they deserve everything they got and more?" Jeremy/Michael was asking him.

"I don't know." Ernie's voice was waning.

"Don't give out on me now, Ernie," Jeremy said. "We're going to see the sun rise again here."

"Michael—"

"Do you have any idea what it was like to be ten years old and wake up in the cold dark, buried alive?

Do you know how scared I was and then finally, how angry? I wish I could have killed them that night."

"But Annie," Ernie was pleading. "She didn't do anything. She wasn't even there."

"You shouldn't have brought her with you, Ernie. This was between me and you. I didn't do anything either," Michael argued. "Where was someone to protect me? Where was my help?"

"So why kill me? We went through the same thing here."

"You knew," Michael told him. "I could tell that you *knew*. I can still take care of Walt, if he survives. You're the last one, Ernie."

Sharyn could make them out in the fast-approaching dawn. The sky was gray enough to see them. They were sitting on the upper-story wall, near the front window. The doors had been gone from this area for a while, along with the windowpanes and some of the walls. There were holes in the ceiling above them letting in the faint light. From somewhere off in the distance, a rooster crowed. The sound was eerie in the predawn silence. Even the wind had died down, leaving only the hard frost continuing to form on the ground, gleaming in the clean morning light.

"No one meant to hurt you, Michael," Ernie told him. "It was stupid but no one meant you to die."

"And I didn't," Michael assured him proudly. "But the three of you will."

"Hold it!" Nick said from across the open room.

Jeremy laughed at him. He picked Ernie up in his strong arms and shoved him against the rotting window frame. "You move and we both go out the window, Nick. You must know that I don't care. I've already been dead once. It was just real cold. So you put down that gun because you can't shoot me without killing both of us. There's a lot of rocks on the ground down there."

Nick put his gun on the floor. It rattled against the old tile. The wind blew in through the cracks in the skeletal frame.

"That's better," Jeremy said. "Now we can all talk about this and decide who should be hurt and who should be avenged!"

When Ernie was safely on the floor again, Sharyn stepped forward. "That's it, Michael." The sound of sirens was clear behind her in the cold morning. Steam rose from her breath as she spoke.

"I don't think so, Sheriff," Michael told her and reached for Ernie again.

Sharyn shot him once in the upper leg. Michael appeared surprised and lost his balance, flailing backward and into the window frame. The momentum took him through the loose wood and plaster.

He fell, clutching a piece of the window frame in his hand. The sound of his body hitting the rocks below was suspended by the noise of the other deputies arriving.

EPILOGUE

"MICHAEL SMITH was beaten up and buried alive by two boys who left him for dead at the old Jefferson Training School forty years ago. Apparently he never forgot or forgave what had happened to him. He killed one of his attackers, Beau Richmond, at the sheriff's office last week. The second, District Court Judge Walter Hamilton, is recovering in the hospital and has identified Smith as the man who attacked him. The sheriff's department has refused comment on a third man who was present at Smith's attack."

Sharyn watched the news from a corner seat at the hospital. The sleek, well-groomed anchorwoman was strolling through the old school grounds where Sharyn had just shot Michael Smith/Jeremy Lambert.

Nick found the child's watch in Jeremy's pocket. There was writing on the back but it would take some work to be able to read it. The small steel club Jeremy had used on his victims was on the frozen ground at his side. Sharyn had left him there and gone with Ernie and Annie to the hospital. Neither one of them were seriously injured. Both were being released and Sharyn was waiting to take them back home.

Michaelson appeared on television briefly, looking harried, rousted roughly from his bed. He only had a few words to say about his job performance in arresting Ernie while the killer was still free. Jack Winter, looking suave and calm as always, had more to say, calling for the ADA's resignation. He answered a few questions briefly, then signaled that he was finished speaking.

"Only one more thing," he said smoothly. "I just want to congratulate Sheriff Sharyn Howard on a job well done. She's truly a force to be reckoned with in Diamond Springs."

He looked at the television camera as though he knew she was watching, and Sharyn shivered. It was nonsense, she knew. She was still cold and exhausted from the trip and confronting Michael Smith. She couldn't go home, though, until things were settled with Ernie.

Ernie and Annie came through the automatic doors from the emergency room together. Annie was white-faced. Her dress was torn in a few places. She held tightly to Ernie's arm.

Ernie was shaken but whole. He held out his hand to Sharyn. She grasped it readily then hugged him tightly to her. "Thanks for waiting."

"I'm so glad you're all right," she told him. "You, too, Annie."

"Thanks, Sheriff," the other woman said quietly.

Sharyn took Ernie's badge out of her pocket. "I'm happy to reinstate you, Deputy Watkins. I've missed you."

Ernie looked at the badge she held out to him, then looked up into her face. "Thanks, Sheriff," he said with a small smile. "But I don't think I can right now."

Sharyn frowned. "You want to take some time off?"

"Not exactly. I don't know if I'll be coming back to the department. My life is different now. I don't know if that's what I want."

She put the badge away and tried not to stare at him. "All right, Ernie. Think about it. There's no hurry."

"Thanks," he said quietly, slipping his arm around Annie.

"I'll drive you home," Sharyn offered, stunned by his refusal to take back his badge.

It was later that night that Nick called and told Sharyn that Frank had found the file for the missing boy. Jeremy Lambert was missing from his parents' home since one Friday afternoon twenty years before. He was never seen again. His dental work matched the remains Beau had dug up from the cemetery. Atlanta police were going to file that he had been killed by Michael Smith and that his body had been transported to North Carolina. Nick was sending the child's bones home for burial. His parents were both still alive and anxious for closure.

Sharyn said good-night and hung up the phone, thanking Nick for letting her know. Her report was going to theorize that Michael Smith had killed Jeremy Lambert and assumed his identity. The reason he'd brought the boy's body to the training school had died with him.

Apparently, he'd become dissatisfied with being "dead," and secure in his new identity, he began blackmailing Judge Hamilton. His decision to come back to Diamond Springs was also a mystery. Sharyn hoped they might clear some of it up when they went through his personal possessions, but she realized that they might never understand what it was like inside his head.

On the desk in her bedroom, the light gleamed dully on Ernie's badge and picked up the bold black print on the invitation that her mother had left for her.

You're invited to the engagement
celebration for
Faye Howard and Senator Caison Talbot
at the Regency Hotel in Diamond Springs.

Sharyn turned off the light and lay down, with her eyes open, staring at the ceiling.

* * * * *